T0209297

Chickenshit

Chickenshit

Everything You Need to Know
but Would Rather Not

Tom Garber

CHICKENSHIT
EVERYTHING YOU NEED TO KNOW BUT WOULD RATHER NOT

iUniverse books may be ordered through booksellers or by contacting:

iUniverse
1663 Liberty Drive
Bloomington, IN 47403
www.iuniverse.com
844-349-9409

Because of the dynamic nature of the Internet, any web addresses or links contained in this book may have changed since publication and may no longer be valid. The views expressed in this work are solely those of the author and do not necessarily reflect the views of the publisher, and the publisher hereby disclaims any responsibility for them.

Any people depicted in stock imagery provided by Getty Images are models, and such images are being used for illustrative purposes only. Certain stock imagery © Getty Images.

ISBN: 978-1-6632-4302-7 (sc)
ISBN: 978-1-6632-4301-0 (e)

Library of Congress Control Number: 2022913604

Print information available on the last page.

iUniverse rev. date: 08/11/2022

Contents

The First Meeting

I didn't even know the Wise Old Chicken existed until my doorbell rang on August 4, 2019. My wife, Anna, was out shopping. I was home alone.

I answered the doorbell but saw no one there. When a stiff peck hit me squarely on the shin, I looked down. There he was. I am not sure of the make or model, Rhode Island whatever, Longhorn this or that ... but he was a rooster, fairly good-sized, totally white with a bright red comb. He could focus his beady eyes into a piercing stare that could melt diamonds.

The best I could do was "Hello." I waited for an egg man or barbecue rep to jump out from the bushes, laughing.

The Wise Old Chicken was not about amusement. Before I could stop him, he marched past me, saying, "You and I gotta talk."

Oh no! I thought. *Don't get feathers on the carpet, don't lay an egg ... don't do that other thing birds do that winds up all gooey and white.* I didn't dare say any of this because he swiveled his head as he went by, holding that beady stare on me like a laser.

I knew roosters didn't lay eggs (duh). I was confused, disturbed that a chicken had entered my home without being invited. What would Anna say? I sniffed the air and could already sense that the house was beginning to smell like a barn. I would have to spray it with an air freshener.

The chicken went to the best chair in the living room (my chair, the one I watch TV in) and hopped onto it. I shut the front door without looking up. I didn't want to see what state my chair might already be in.

"Sit down on the couch," the chicken said. "I don't have much time."

I sat down, dumbfounded.

The chicken continued his frightful stare. "You're the nut trying to find out about URA," he said.

This made me grin. "You got me," I said. "Did I call you?"

"I wouldn't smile, young man. You are in a shitload of trouble."

He was referring to a bit of fun I'd been having the past few days. Anna and I had retired from our "real jobs" recently, and I played with the idea that there existed something I called the usual retirement age or the URA.

Some people knew me as a minor writer of the times. I had sold several short stories. These tales were nothing special, just something that might interest a few others here and there. All my stories dealt in the ridiculous ways that haughty and obnoxious people were brought down a peg or two.

I had been a bit on the sassy side of humanity, a semiprofessional tease. Just for fun, you see.

With my newfound free time, I had taken on the challenge of using my talents to keep our planet on a steady keel and not let things get too snotty, my word for "haughty conceit."

My purpose was to annoy my fellow man whenever possible … in a good way. I suppose you could say that I had now moved onto the professional arena. My only worries were how to keep from getting punched in the nose and how to stay out of jail.

The URA worked perfectly for my purposes. I checked online, and sure enough, my acronym ran with some of the big boys: Uganda Revenue Authority, uniformly redundant array, upper removable appliance. I would have been happy to allow Undulating Residual Adversaries, Ugly Rear Assembly, or even the Ultimate Righteous Assholes (of America). I was quite pleased with my embryo of botheration.

Anna and I lived near the tight little city of Knoxville. Oak Ridge, that bastion of national secrecy, was only a stone's throw beyond. Innumerable universities and colleges were in the area.

I decided to make a few trial runs with my new toy, and test the reaction of academia. To decrease universal snot, there was no better place to start. Not many in the scholarly world cared to admit ignorance of anything, an important seed to the overall problem.

I got through to a professor on my first call. I asked him, "How does one go about calculating their own URA?"

After a long pause, I heard, "URA." (This was a statement, not a question.)

"Yes," I said.

There was another pause before his phone crashed down on my ear. I waited until I heard the dial tone again to confirm the dastardly thing I had suspected. My first try had gone pretty well.

No matter what school leaders I called, I got the same response. I decided to throw caution to the wind and began calling offices in Oak Ridge. Results: the same. My ear was getting happily fatigued by the sound of crashing receivers. I was having a marvelous time.

In my living room, the chicken broke my reverie with a rather unnerving question. "Do you actually know anything about URA?"

I felt like John Cleese with my mouth hanging open in a scene out of *Fawlty Towers*. I said, "It just means 'Usual Retirement Age.' I made it up. For fun."

"You have a strange idea of fun, my boy," the chicken said. "Tell me, have you or anyone you know been to Europe lately? Moscow?"

Now I felt the first pangs of serious alarm. "What the hell," I said. "What does it really mean, URA?"

The chicken shook his head. "You don't have to know."

"Give me a break," I said. "It was only a joke."

"You know we are going to check your travel records."

With that he stood and walked by me to the door, again turning his head to keep me fixed in his gaze. "You haven't seen the last of me," he said, opening the door and closing it sharply behind him.

I was aghast.

Then I saw something lying on the chair where the old bird had been sitting: a thick satchel. Under his fixed gaze, I hadn't noticed that the chicken had brought something with him. I grabbed the bag and headed to the door as fast as I could.

The chicken had disappeared. I stepped out onto the lawn and looked up and down the street. No cars, no one walking. I heard a helicopter receding into the distance but thought to myself, *Nah! Can't be.*

As I said before, I had no idea who the Wise Old Chicken was. All I knew about him was from moments before. I would prefer not to make him angry again anytime soon.

But I held his satchel.

I went back inside and sat in my chair. It was immaculately clean. The chicken had left no barnyard refuse. The house smelled fine. I wouldn't have to spray.

Under the rules that guided my quest to simplify the world, going through a stranger's belongings was acceptable, sometimes imperative. I opened the satchel. Inside were a number of written pages, notes on various Wise Old Chicken adventures.

I knew that I was guilty only of trying to tease. But my visit from the Wise Old Chicken had unnerved me. I tossed all traces of my acronym notes into the trash. I had no idea what URA really meant, and now I never wanted to know.

In several days, a note found its way to my doorstep. It said simply: "I know your game. See what it's like to deal with you? Ha, ha. P.S. Left the notes on purpose. Hope you can do them justice. Thanks, WOC."

The stories in this book have been written accordingly. If the old buzzard shows up again, we'll most likely have a great time. I hope.

The End

The Man Who Mowed Too Much

Don't assume what you think you are told.

There once was a man who lived with his wife in a small village at the edge of many wide fields. The couple had a pretty little cottage with a green lawn and cascades of roses of all descriptions. In the fields grew wheat, barley, and flax.

The man had met many testy strangers who strode by the village, seeking him from afar because of his rather peculiar reputation. Everyone called him "the man who mowed too much."

A visitor would ask the man a question like this: "What exactly do you mow best?"

The man would scratch his grizzly jaw as he thought. "I suppose I mow small mammals best, them that lives in the fields."

Trying as best he could, the stranger kept his horror to himself. But he had to know the truth, what to tell his friends once he returned home. The newcomer asked, "Why would you mow small animals?"

"I suppose because they are just there," the man would explain. "When I work in the fields the little creatures are everywhere."

The newcomer might grimace, but would still ask, "Is there anything else that you might mow?"

"Oh, I mow lots of things," the man has been known to say. "I mow birds. I mow reptiles, snakes, lizards, and turtles, that sort of thing. I mow trees ..."

"You mow trees?"

"Yes, I certainly do! Elms. Hickories. And oaks, huge oaks. All them that grows 'round here."

Of course, as you might expect, visitors almost always gave up at this point and went unhappily on their way.

"If it means anything," the man would call out after them, "I'm fluent in seven different languages."

The man was not sure why new folks treated him so.

Then his wife called out, "Honey, did you mow that it's almost time for lunch?"

"No, dear," the man said. "Thanks for letting me mow that."

"We have a guest, dear," she added. "The Wise Old Chicken has paid us a visit."

Before everyone sat down to eat, the chicken asked the man, "So, what do you mow these days?"

"Eh, about the usual," the man said. "Not much more than when we last met."

As they consumed a most magnificent lunch of roast beef, potatoes, and broccoli soup, the chicken described his latest adventures, to the man and his wife's delight.

Afterward, the chicken had to be on his way. The man escorted his friend out to the front porch. On the lawn before them, the grass was long and straggly.

The Wise Old Chicken said, in good humor, "Looks like someone needs to trim their lawn …"

"I mow," the man said.

The End

The Tree That Couldn't Fly

Don't do anything dangerous until you know how to do it, duh.

One day a bushy young tree was flying high above the land. The wind was lovely and cool, and all the tree's leaves were shaking with glee. The tree was just learning to fly and had taken to the sky without its instructor's approval.

What is everyone afraid of? the tree thought gaily. *This is so easy.*

Beneath the tree passed a miniature world—tiny trees, houses, and fields. Hills and ridges spread in every direction, as far as the eye could see.

Finally, the tree grew tired. Flying for any sort of plant is a drafty business. Several of the young tree's leaves had blown off, and its roots were getting a bit too dry. It spied a pleasant forest below.

Time to land, the tree told itself. *I will descend ever so gently at the edge of that forest. And I see a babbling brook down there, a nice moist spot where my roots can get a good drink.*

Anyone experienced with the countryside would have known that the "brook" was, in fact, a raging cataract that cut through a deep gorge, far below the level of the forest.

With confidence, the tree started down.

Now it so happened that a wise old chicken was walking carefully along the same forest's edge, along a rocky path that bordered the steep cliff to the frothing rapids below.

Hearing a *whoosh* overhead, which grew louder by the second, the chicken looked up.

"Struth!" the chicken said out loud. He recognized the tree descending above him and winced. He was acquainted with the tree's flight instructor and knew that the tree had not yet learned to land properly, even if there was a runway present.

"It doesn't know what it's doing!" the chicken cried out. "It doesn't know the first thing about landing!" Then, "Great Caesar's Ghost! It's coming right down on top of me."

Just in time, the chicken leaped away from the path so it could watch from beneath the safety of the forest canopy.

The tree hurtled down, bounced once on its roots on the rocky path, and, with a heartfelt cry, disappeared over the edge of the cliff. The chicken peered over and saw the tree in all its leafiness being swept away in the swift current of the river until it went out of sight around the first bend.

It has been said that the tree was washed all the way to the ocean, where it sank to the deepest part and was never seen again.

The tree should not have been flying on its own, the old chicken thought sadly.

The wise old bird sighed. *Poor tree. It simply assumed too much for itself. Why is it that young people these days have so little patience? Will they ever learn?*

The End

The Red Birds and
the Green Trees

A flock of bright red birds fluttered down into a thicket of extraordinarily green trees. The treetops were so lush the birds could hide almost anywhere and still watch the sky above and peer down into the dark forest floor below. The birds happily agreed with one another that they had arrived at the very best place to be invisible to predators.

Unfortunately, the birds were all color-blind. Their entire species had this affliction. Each bird saw the world the same as every one of the others. Not one of them knew the truth: that they all stood out in the greenery like beacons.

From the treetops, the only predators that the birds had to worry about were the wandering packs of carnivorous giraffes.

The birds did not realize that a dozen or so of the loathsome creatures were barely a mile away, working across the open savanna in a feeding frenzy, plucking up, biting, swallowing, and delighting themselves with any creature the size of a hyena or smaller, whether it hopped, ran, or slithered.

It was a hideous sight. The carnivorous giraffes smiled to congratulate one another on their fine repast. Blood dripped from fangs that remained visible when their mouths were closed, much like the teeth of a crocodile. This was one of the features that made a carnivorous giraffe look *slightly* different than a normal giraffe.

Their other distinguishing ability was a telescoping neck. These animals strode about with their heads about the same height as a normal giraffe. But when needed, they could stalk the tops of the tallest trees, pouncing, as it were, down into the foliage from above and eating the prey that had been looking for trouble from below.

The giraffes were not color-blind.

The red birds, settling into their newly discovered hiding place, told each other in confidence, "Nobody will ever find us here."

A stern voice came from far below. "I wouldn't get too relaxed."

It was a wise old chicken who, gasping for breath, had just entered the dark, shadowy ground. He took a deep breath and called out to the birds again, "I just had to duck and sprint around several carnivorous giraffes. I don't know if they saw me, but they're getting close to here!"

The chicken had known the birds a long time. He had no idea about their problems in perceiving color because the subject never had a reason to present itself. The chicken *did* know that this flock of red birds was the last on earth. He never had the heart to tell them what evolution had in store for them.

"Hah!" one of the red birds called down. "They'll never spot us up here."

The chicken couldn't understand why the birds were not concerned. They could be cocky, but this was ridiculous. Probably one reason they were on the brink of extinction.

The chicken drew the line at interfering with evolution. He would not get in nature's way. On the other hand, he had his own safety to consider. (It would be several years before the chicken became so proficient in martial arts that he never feared another threat of any kind.)

"I'd better get along," he called up into the trees. "I really suggest that you birds do the same."

The chicken, having caught his breath, began to jog through the shade and soon found himself running over the open ground until he was a safe distance from the trees.

Not two minutes later, the first giraffe walked under the boughs, followed by the others. The birds all hushed, some of them choking back giggling fits over how clever they were being. They looked down on the giraffes' bodies and spindly legs. A few of the necks had already stretched out of sight above the foliage. Without warning, crocodile teeth descended among them from above, and the first birds disappeared in single bites.

In the distance, the Wise Old Chicken heard the last groans and screams of the red birds. They were now officially extinct. The chicken also listened to the giraffes belching and laughing like ghouls. The chicken turned to hurry on his way.

Evolution has got to do better than that, he thought.

Glancing up at the sky above, he said out loud, "That's just my opinion, you understand."

Just in case …

The End

The Saga of the Colt
and the Bull

Early one dewy morning, when the sun was just getting high enough in the sky to promise its coming warmth, a little colt scampered up a hill.

While the picture of this young foal was as agreeable to the heart as a basket of kittens, we do feel it prudent to note some of the peculiarities we have observed as our little friend cantered happily on his way.

Take, for instance, the way his head rocked not only up and down, as you would expect of any young horse. This colt's head rocked from side to side as well, even when he stopped to take a breath. He had large eyes that rolled all over the place, each in opposite directions. He had a slightly protruding tongue that covered a constantly grinning lower lip so that a plume of spittle floated out every time he spoke.

If someone said that the colt had a screw loose, be assured such a comment did not come from us. We prefer you, dear reader, to be your own judge. Surely, we must not be too harsh on young creatures that seem somewhat different from others of their kind. After all, they may have a rough road ahead of them, and they may need all the assistance they can get.

Someone used the term "whackadoo." This *did not* come from us.

"Oh, would that I could run to the very top of the hill, and that's just what I'll do, I'll do do do," the little colt sang in a quavering high-pitched voice, spittle flying every which way. "A boon for me and a boon for thee, perchance we find along the way, the way, the way … Wheeee!"

At the top of the hill, the colt came upon a wrinkly old bull lying under a large tree. The bull was lifelong bone-tired, and the air was cool and damp under the tree for now. But later, once the noonday sun had climbed to the top of the sky and began to sear the land with its summer heat, the old bovine was in the perfect spot to enjoy the shade.

This bull had had a long, "hard" life doing what bulls are supposed to do. Now he had finished his work. All he desired was peace and to be left alone.

And here, out of the blue, appeared this colt, prancing around him, head rocking, large eyes rolling, a tongue flopping about, and a plume of spittle spraying at every sound that issued from his silly mouth.

"Pray," spat the colt, merrily. "May that I might receive a boon from thee, from thee, from thee ... Huh?"

"Boon?" sighed the bull. "What in hell are you talking about? Do you mean a bone, a bun? Go away, I don't have any bones or buns to give you."

"No, a boon, a boon, a boon!" squealed the colt happily, jumping this way and that.

The old bull watched the frisky colt's movements. But the youngster moved too quickly for the bull to watch all of it because the old boy was not inclined to lift and turn his head fast enough to keep up. Consequently, what the bull saw was this insane little creature popping in and out of view. The quavering little laugh seemed to fill the sky. Happy little jets of spittle filled the air.

The bull said to himself, *Here I am, desiring only peace— and I get this nutball?*

Suddenly the colt jumped to a stop, though still wiggling his head. "Would that I could gain some of your great wisdom. Pray that I might have this very boon! Puulleeze …"

As he said this, the colt stuck his wobbling head directly into the bull's face. The bull recoiled when he felt the sprinkling from the colt's mouth.

The bull took a long hard look at the colt. He thought, *Walks like a nut, talks like a nut … The kid is demented. Boon? Why me, Lord?*

The colt stared back with his enormous rolling eyes. His mouth hung open in a slack smile. He couldn't stop wiggling his head.

Just then, the old bull felt more than slightly unwell. He thought that this could be "the big one," and he was surprised to find that he could care less, given his present predicament. It was a good way out.

"Boy, you want my wisdom?" the bull groaned. "Well, here it is. Stop saying 'boon.' And stop talking like an idiot."

And with that, the old bull rolled onto its back, wiggled its hooves in the air, and died.

"Bull?" sang the colt. "Oh, bull."

But the old bull said nothing because he was dead. Being dead, it was rather hard for him to answer, not that it meant much to the colt.

It was as if the colt didn't understand what had happened. He pranced around and sang, "Old bull go sleepy. Tired old bull. And when the bough breaks … and when the bough breaks … uhhh." The colt couldn't remember how the rest of that went, so he simply grinned and wobbled his head. "The boon, the boon …"

"Colt! What have you done to this poor bull?" came an angry voice behind the youngster.

The colt turned to see a wise old chicken looking sternly at him. The chicken had been the bull's longtime friend.

The colt's mouth dropped open in delight. "From thee I pray!" he cried out happily, with an extra spit for good measure. "From thee the very boon for me? A boon for me?"

"Boon?" the chicken said, now slightly perplexed. "You mean a bone? A bun?"

"No, a boon!" came the goofy reply.

The chicken eyed the colt carefully and began to get a fairly good idea of all that had just transpired. He sighed and shook his head. Then he pointed down to the bottom of the hill with a wing.

"See that pretty pasture down there?" the chicken said gently. "Lots of nice fresh grass. And soon it will be noon, you'll have lots of nice sunshine. Why don't you be a good little fellow and trot down there and frolic about?"

The colt shrugged, nodded eagerly with his eyes rolling, and ran off. "No boon. No boon today," he cried merrily, sputtering spit as he went. "Perhaps in the pasture a boon for me, a boon for thee, or so we will find, oh whee, whee, whee!"

"And from now on," the chicken said under his breath, "please keep as far away from me as you possibly can."

Synopsis of our story so far: No boon will come to a loon who does not attune for his lack of a spittoon even while trying to croon his own goony tune well before noon. Such a loon makes all others swoon and want to get to the nearest saloon.

How did the rest of the story go? Well …

The chicken ordered a large hearse to take the bull decently and mercifully away. The chicken then checked with all the vet and county records and, to his amazement, found that the bull had inseminated no less than an incredible number of 345,412⅔ cows.

The bull had been in business for a remarkable twelve full years. He averaged seventy-nine cows a day. Of course, he rested on some days, and on others had to work on overdrive the keep up the average.

Long speeches at the funeral lauded the great feat. Everyone was flabbergasted. They all chipped in to have a giant memorial stone specially carved in the bull's honor and erected (read: quite erect) at the top of the grave. Decorum prevents us from a description of this monument in much detail. Suffice it to say that it rose high above the ground and took most people's breath away when they first came upon it.

As for the colt, all that the chicken knew was that the last time he looked down toward the paddock below, he saw the colt chasing after a group of three adult horses and two cows. All five seemed to be running for their lives with the colt hot on their tails. The chicken didn't wait around to see how the race ended.

The End

The Old Couple Who Wanted to Improve Their View

Once upon a time, an old man and his wife lived on the side of a hill that overlooked the treetops of a forest below, providing a lovely view of mountains in the distance. The old couple loved the leafy green trees, and they cherished the mountains. They were so happy with their view that they never missed a chance to show it off when visitors dropped by. Everyone stood at the window and agreed that it was the most wonderful view for miles around.

But over the years, the hillside below their home began to change. The youngest trees at the edge of the forest did what young trees everywhere do. They grew. And they grew. Before the old couple's sad and unbelieving eyes, the mountains slowly began to disappear.

Finally, the wonderful view was gone. The old couple stood at their window in sorrow. All they saw were trees, which were beautiful themselves. Their precious view would never return.

One day the old man sighed and told his wife there was nothing left for it—he would have to chop some trees down. It would be a lot of work, and especially hard on the old couple's hearts since they had always felt such affection for the trees. They both agreed that the work had to be done.

Just then, their doorbell rang. Outside was a chicken. The man and his wife were elated; they had heard that a very wise old chicken had been in the vicinity, going around and giving advice on all sorts of things. Possibly (hopefully, most certainly?) the couple's problems might now be solved some other way.

"I understand you are having a problem with your view," the chicken said. "If you would be so kind as to let me come in, I can make a few suggestions that might be of some use."

The old couple invited the chicken in. He went immediately to the window where the trees obscured the mountain view.

The chicken studied the problem for a long time. He looked this way and that and made tiny clucking sounds, and again and again muttered, "Hmm ..."

Suddenly the chicken turned to the couple and announced, "I am prepared to make three proposals to solve the problem!"

The man and his wife looked at each other and tried but failed to keep from breaking into wide smiles, their eyes beginning to tear.

"First," the chicken said, "have you thought of draping a rather large canvas over the trees? Upon this surface, you could paint the mountains. Why, a talented artist could craft something as good as the real thing."

The man and his wife looked at each other again; the smiles had turned straight, and their eyes questioned each other.

Seeing that this idea was not all that well-received, the chicken quickly said, "Okay, okay. Then here is my second thought."

The old couple sighed, somewhat relieved, and were all ears.

The chicken began carefully. "There is an airport within ten miles of here, is there not?"

The couple both nodded.

"And at that airport, there is a helicopter?"

"Yes, that is true," said the man.

The chicken, intently studying the view, let his eyes go half-closed and now spoke in a faraway voice, as if in a trance. "We shall simply rent the helicopter and a pilot ... yesss ... this should work ... but it must be a good pilot, good indeed. We will simply instruct the pilot to fly the helicopter upside down ... low, quite low, over the treetops ... so that the rotor chops all the branches away ... cuts it all down as low as you want ... right to the ground."

The chicken snapped his fingers. "Now, how's that?"

Again the old man and the old woman did not reply, as many readers might readily expect.

"What! Don't like that idea?" the chicken suddenly snapped, turning to look fiercely at them. "You two seem quite hard to please."

"Well," said the old man, timidly because of the sudden outburst. "What is your third suggestion? You said you had three."

The chicken stood back. "My third idea? Why, my third idea is the finest of them all," he replied, rather grandly.

The chicken turned his head and looked sideways at each of them. Then he fastened them with his eyes opening wide, his beak contorting into a warped grin. "My third idea is pure genius, utterly simple, it cannot be surpassed. You are going to be amazed that you had not thought of this before."

The man and his wife both gulped. "Go on."

The chicken shook his head, the wild look growing in his eyes.

"Just put in taller mountains!"

At this point, the chicken began singing to them. "Lu-cukoo lu-cukoo-la-dee-la-da …"

The man was indignant. "I am surprised that such a wise old chicken can only come up with such nonsense."

The chicken stopped his song and grinned at him. "What wise old chicken? I'm not a wise old chicken. In fact, I'm crazy as a loon. Whatever made you think I was wise? Lu-kee-lu-do-a-dee-la-da …" he sang, bobbing his head like a turkey.

At that very moment, the actual Wise Old Chicken happened by the old folks' home on the road out front. *This used to be a wonderful view*, he thought. *Someone really should chop down those damn trees.*

The chicken proceeded on his way.

The End

Trees in the Forest

Deep in the forest, three saplings had sprouted near a fourth tree that was middle-aged.

The older tree was delighted to have the three newcomers growing close enough for them to hear and speak to one another. And as our story begins, it so happened that the four often engaged in earnest and friendly discussions.

Now, before we continue, someone might ask, "Trees can talk?"

This is quite a reasonable question. Most folks think that trees do not talk. On the contrary, they most certainly do. But the thing is, they speak very slowly, painfully slowly, so intolerably slowly that no one has time to wait long enough to hear what they have to say.

As an example, a tree might say to its neighbor, "I must say, I really like our forest. Does it agree with you?"

It would take five or ten years to complete those two sentences, perhaps more. Then another five years or so for a short reply. Who but a tree has the time to wait that long?

Understandably, trees have a terrible sense of time compared with the rest of the world. They have no idea how many years they have been around.

Now, dear reader, we must let you in on a secret. We have written this tale in tree speech. This is for the benefit of any tree that might want to read our work. While you read the above paragraphs, all four trees had grown over a hundred years. The three young trees were now middle-aged, and the older tree was nearing the end of its days.

The old tree's boughs ached so badly it could no longer remember how nice a fresh breeze felt. The wind pushed its limbs and made them hurt worse. The old tree couldn't always keep all its leaves throughout the summer. It was embarrassing.

The three younger trees were considering a question they had all heard before, several "days" ago: "When a tree falls in the forest and nobody is around, does the falling tree make a noise?"

The young trees held that there would, in fact, be quite a loud crash, no matter who was around. Why would physics change so abruptly, as if on a whim, to stop the process of sound?

The old tree was fed up with listening to this drivel. It did not want to hear about old trees dying in the first place. And in the second place, it did not want to imagine a dead tree falling and becoming a mossy log rotting on the ground.

"Of course there's no sound," the old tree said. "Have you ever heard a tree fall? No, you haven't. Now, can't we talk about something more agreeable?" The old tree sighed.

"But why wouldn't there be any sound?" one of the younger trees pressed on.

"Stop this talk!" the old tree said, huffing loudly. It had had enough of this discussion.

"But we just don't understand," a young tree tried to explain, quite reasonably, without thinking of the old one's feelings. "When a tree falls ... it's huge, and it falls all the way down from its full height and hits the ground so hard—surely, you must hear something."

Sometime during the years it took for this statement to be made, the old tree spoke again. It shook its few remaining leaves in uncontrolled rage. Its sap boiled and burst through its veins; its bark fell in slabs from its trunk. It shouted, "You should not ... uhhh!"

With a great shiver and a gasp, the old tree died.

"Oh, I say," one of the other trees said.

"I fear the worst has happened," said another.

By the time the younger trees finished talking, the old tree had rotted into a dry trunk with only a few broken stubs as boughs. They never saw the dead tree begin to list until its stump crumbled and the entire carcass fell to the ground. To them, the old trunk had been upright one moment, and the next it was a mossy old log on the ground.

Of course, the younger trees had heard nothing. "So now we know," they all said, reverently.

"Listen," said one, "we've had a good conversation. But for myself, I have errands to run, places to go, and things to do."

"Yes. I suppose we must be going too," the others said.

All three tried to heave themselves this way and that. But it was no use. Obviously, they remained rooted where they were. "Eergg, oooff, uughh, arrghh," they all said, trying to pull free.

To anyone else, this struggle was not apparent. They saw nothing but three trees standing majestically with their leaves fluttering in the breeze.

Just then, a wise old chicken came along and stopped. He *was* fluent in tree speech and able to watch, just barely, in tree time. He saw enough to know exactly what the trees were trying to do.

"Trees," sighed the chicken. "Always yakking about something. They talk so damn much they forget what they are."

The chicken shook his head and continued on his way, leaving the futile struggle behind. He had many more important things to do.

The End

A Little Fish on
a Big Beach

In some tropical latitudes, sparkling warm oceans meet island shores of brilliant white sand. Small, gentle waves march in with metronomic regularity, rarely breaking, to glide up the sand no more than a few feet before washing back. At the top of the sand thickets of sea grapes, their flat green leaves the size of saucers and translucent in the bright sunshine, tremble in the cool daytime breezes that follow the waves of the sea.

Our story begins close to one of these shores, where an enormous school of small fish streaks through the crystal water in a twisting, churning, and ever-moving ballet. Each fish follows the movements of the others, quickly turning this way and that without warning. The changing movements ripple through the school so that one might see many fish going one way, against a background of countless others heading in various opposing directions.

The small fish do this instinctively, to present a confounding myriad of patterns to predators. The swirling mass makes it almost impossible for a larger fish to focus on a single target.

The multitude of little fish also provides a grim kind of protection for the whole—safety in numbers. The more individuals there are, the less chance that any particular one will be eaten. If one or two disappear, the loss to the whole is insignificant.

Such is life in the particular school that we are about to tell you about.

Among this darting mass, a restless little fish swam in perfect unison with his neighbors, just as he had done all his life. It was becoming such a bore.

"Why do we swim like this all day?" he asked himself out loud, irritably, knowing the answer anyway.

"For our own good," said a more sensible fish nearby.

"That may be as well for you and the others," the restless fish said. "But I believe I will try something new."

The school suddenly cut to the left, toward the open water. The restless fish went right, toward the beach. He hadn't gotten six inches before a large set of jaws came up from behind.

The teeth behind him snapped shut, but the small fish shot clear at the last moment and launched himself up onto the sand, exactly where he wanted to go.

Deliriously happy, the little fish realized where he was. He pushed himself up to stand on the tips of his tail and waved his pectorals like little arms. Dancing in a little circle, he shouted with joy. "Zoweee!"

Then, his little arm fins pumping madly, he began running along the sand. "Yippee-doo, yippee-doo," he cried in happiness.

He was having so much fun he failed to notice a seagull taking a mighty interest from far above and behind him.

But then, seeing the growing shadow of the diving gull, the fish hopped sideways at the last moment so that the toothy bill closed with a mighty clack over a foot away.

"Ha!" laughed the fish, and ran faster, zigging and zagging. "Yippee-doo. Hoohaa," he sang.

The noise awakened a decrepit old beach cat. The cat had been sound asleep in the flickering shadows beneath the sea grapes. She roused her aching joints slowly and went into a trembling crouch. The fish shot by, and the cat sprang, missing by a good four feet.

To hell with it, the cat thought, returning to her resting place. *How ridiculous was that?*

The fish continued along its merry way. "Yahaaa yahoo!" he squealed, feinting this way and that, pirouetting and doing cartwheels.

Now, unbeknownst to the fish, up ahead were two high-speed land racing crabs. This type of crab could easily outpace a greyhound. Consequently, these crabs had long since been banned from dog racing. They complicated betting odds too much.

Racing crabs have ridiculously long eye stalks so that they can see farther ahead when at speed. They were able to see the little fish coming long before he knew they were there. They crouched in the sand on either side of the fish's path.

"Yahoo!" the little fish laughed, unaware of the approaching ambush.

The crabs charged, immediately at full sprint. The fish shot between them. Before the crabs could turn in pursuit, they crashed together so hard that all four eye stalks twirled into a tangle of knots. It would take them hours to sort things out.

Having run so fast and so far, the little fish was now tired and becoming rather dry.

"Foof!" he said. "I will jump back into the sea."

He ran down the slope of the sand and leaped into the first little wave. He swam a bit and as luck would have it, he came upon the very school he had left. He inserted himself into the outside position he had enjoyed before and once again began moving as one with all the others.

"I'm back!" the fish called excitedly to his neighbor.

"Oh?" the neighboring fish replied. "I didn't know you had gone anywhere." (This response was directly related to the school's ability to carry on as if nothing happened whenever it lost a few of its numbers.)

The little fish was rather deflated by this comment. But it made him think.

I suppose, he thought as he swam along with the group, *it might make a lot more sense to stay with the school. My jaunt was exhilarating, but it certainly was dangerous. After all, here I have safety in numbers.*

No sooner had he had this thought than a big fish plucked our small friend and his neighbor neatly from the rest. The large fish turned, swallowed once, and was gone. Both little fish were no more.

The rest of the school went on its way—hundreds of fish swerving and turning, all quite unaware they were now two less. And everything went on as it should.

Now at that very moment, on the surface of the water, a wise old chicken rowed his little boat parallel to the shore. He had seen and understood everything that had happened. The chicken shook his head and thought, *Sometimes it's hard to find a moral. I guess you could say that you must keep within your boundaries, live the life you are supposed to live and let the coins fall where they may. But what a downer!*

The chicken pulled on the oars and soon came to a crowded martini bar, built right out on the sand. *A rum punch would go nicely just about now*, he thought.

The End

The Mushroom Who Loved Bobby Pins

In the soft leafy mulch under the forest trees, a little mushroom popped into being. He took a deep breath and sighed with happiness at feeling the cool air and at being alive. His name was Jimmy.

Fungi generally are not known for their piercing brainpower. Jimmy particularly so. A hint of toadstool had corrupted his genes sometime in the past. This was due to either a mating or other spore interchange that had gone horribly wrong, or other nefarious activity that surely involved liquor and shame.

Jimmy was a busy little beastie. No more than ten minutes after having poked his round little head above the ground, Jimmy had made up his mind as to what he wanted more than anything else. Bobby pins. *Bobby pins!* The things girls and women put in their hair.

Like any other young mushroom, Jimmy had no more hair than a smooth river stone. Who knows where he got his ideas? Men wearing bobby pins! Maybe it was a hippie thing.

The little mushroom spent his first day wishing as hard as he could for bobby pins. All he could do was yearn into the forest air and think, *Bobby pins … bobby pins …*

Presently, night fell, and the exhausted mushroom was soon asleep. And behold, when he felt the warm sun on him the next day, he opened his eyes to find next to him a neat stack of the very things he had wished for—bobby pins!

All Jimmy could think was that a fairy had heard his wishes and fulfilled them.

"Oh, good fairy, dear, precious fairy, thank you, from the bottom of my heart," Jimmy said out loud, with all the reverence he could muster.

Suddenly, a wise old chicken was there, towering over the ground and eyeing the little mushroom.

"What are you yammering about?" the chicken asked.

When the mushroom excitedly told the chicken all about what had happened, the chicken had a good idea of what he was dealing with. The chicken had come across many strange things in his travels. This was a first.

The old bird didn't have the heart to tell our little friend that there was no fairy involved. The truth was that squirrels often absconded with bobby pins from the shipping department of a bobby pin factory. More to the point, the bobby pin factory was *less than* one hundred yards beyond the forest edge.

The bushy-tailed heathens piled their loot next to mushrooms because they knew that the soil there was soft and easy to dig. Something must have interrupted that night's proceedings. The squirrels had scampered back into their trees. They would probably bury their loot the next night.

"What are squirrels? Why do they want bobby pins?" the mushroom asked.

"Squirrels are fuzzy creatures, yea long." The chicken held his wingtips appropriately apart. Suddenly he had to jerk one wing against his side as if something had almost fallen out.

"Squirrels have fluffy tails, and the proud little bandits like to show off. They manicure themselves with the bobby pins. They preen endlessly and show off one extravagant style after another.

"This goes on even during winter, when the squirrels dig up nuts they'd buried when it was warmer. They also dig up caches of bobby pins if it gets too cold to make a run on the factory."

The mushroom listened politely, but the chicken could see tears beginning to drip from its button.

The chicken sighed. It would be pointless to explain further. *What the hey*, the chicken thought. *The little guy wanted bobby pins. So now he's got bobby pins.*

"I want to put bobby pins in my hair," whispered Jimmy. Then he stopped short. "But I don't have any hair!"

The chicken shook its head. He resolved to help the little mushroom, even though it was entirely against his, the chicken's, nature, as we will see plainly in a moment.

"Don't despair," the chicken said. "You do have hair. It's just that it is not on your head."

"Where is it, then?"

"It's all around you. Underground. Your mycelium, roots. Enormous amounts, more than any head of hair that I've ever seen."

That did it. Jimmy was delighted and tried to jump up and down. He couldn't do this, but that didn't worry him. "Could you help me, then?" the mushroom asked.

The chicken was prepared to do whatever the little mushroom wanted. First he walked into the trees and hid something under his wing beneath a bush.

When the chicken returned, Jimmy happily directed exactly where he wanted each pin positioned. The chicken would pick up a bobby pin in its beak and wait for Jimmy's instructions.

"Put one there. Another one there. One there." Jimmy was having the time of his life.

One by one the chicken stuck each forked end into the ground as the little mushroom bade him. The pins stood in a curve that began to spiral out from the mushroom at its center. The little mushroom laughed and sang. Squirrels heard the commotion and crept down from the trees to see what was happening.

The Wise Old Chicken returned to the bush in the trees and picked up the parcel he had hidden before. As Jimmy's voice faded in the distance, the chicken brought out a paper bag that bulged with mushrooms. And licked his beak.

But the story had only begun, and the chicken would learn the truth years later. He traveled back to the same woods and began searching the area where he remembered that the mushroom had lived.

The mushroom was gone, of course. There were no mushrooms anywhere in the area. The chicken wondered if some disease had affected the mycelium underground.

The chicken knew that he had come to the correct place. Before him, *thousands* of bobby pins were stuck in the ground. Each pin, now rusting in the elements, continued the spiral pattern far from the center where the little mushroom had sung.

The squirrels told the old bird that they were so taken by the mushroom's happiness that no one was going to clean up the original loops, even after the mushroom was gone.

The area was now the squirrels' special venue for weddings. Each couple left one bobby pin to mark the day they had become one. So far, all those couples who followed this ritual were blessed with happy marriages and plenty of children.

In this way, the squirrels honored the memory of a simple mushroom, and by extension, all the joys of life. It was a happy thing. The ceremony would continue until the end of time.

The End

Millipede Mathematics

Ructions before the big game

A millipede named Lester sat at his kitchen table and threw back a double of Dead Possum Scotch. The label on the bottle called it scotch. It was the cheapest rotgut money could buy, conjured up in places like Squirmy Town, Iowa, or Mad Dog, New Mexico. There were a few who liked it, many more who did not. "It is an acquired … taste," the former group told the latter.

Lester was fortifying himself against the chance that he had lost a leg. He had come across a loose millipede leg in the forest and had carried it home to put on his living room couch for closer examination. The leg was the same size as Lester's; it wore a red tennis shoe that was just like his many others.

Today of all days. His longtime Ping-Pong rival, a centipede called Billy the Basher, was due in a couple of hours for a match to settle once and for all who was the best.

The only way Lester could be sure that he was all there was to count the number of legs he had left. He was too anxious to count all the way up to one thousand. He had tried but had already lost track a dozen times. More Dead Possum was the only thing he knew to calm his nerves.

He was positive Billy the Basher had something to do with all this. Just a sneaky way to gain an advantage during the big match.

His doorbell rang, and Lester shouted, "Door's open."

In walked the Wise Old Chicken. He had come a long way to watch the contest. He had never witnessed multilegged arthropods playing table tennis. He shook the dust from his feathers and exhaled long and loud, to dramatize his exhaustion. Then he got himself a glass, sat across from Lester, and poured himself a good double.

The chicken threw it back. "Pahhh. Hits the spot," he said. He poured himself another and leaned back in his chair. "What's going on? You look worried."

Lester told the chicken what had happened, showed him the disembodied leg lying on his couch, and explained his suspicions of Billy.

"Why are you sure it's yours?"

"It's wearing one of my sneakers."

The chicken looked closely. "Well, it's red, like yours. A 'Li'l Bug'. Sized …" The chicken tried to read the dirty and scuffed label. "1/16!"

"That's *my* size," said Lester. "And nobody wears red. I had to look all over town to find one thousand. Once I bought mine, I was told that there were no red shoes left."

(The reason a millipede can afford to buy one shoe, let alone one thousand, is because of the Federal Multi Leg Arthropod Shoe Act of 1969. Not all millipedes purchase shoes; some still prefer to go *au naturel*. But enough individuals make use of the FMLASA to give America's economy a friendly nudge.)

Lester said, "I need to see I still have one thousand legs. That's the only way I can be sure."

"What makes you think you started with one thousand?"

"Because *I'm* a millipede!" Lester said. He turned and drew a great tome from his cupboard and slammed it on the table.

Interested, the chicken read the title. "*The Big Book of Millipedes and What They Should Not Know Until of Age.*" He opened the book and began to read.

"Lester, it says here that millipedes don't actually have one thousand legs. Some have only several hundred …"

"What?"

"Let's see about how many you really have."

The chicken did a quick count of a quarter of one side of Lester's body. "72," the chicken said. "That means you have, let's see … 72 x 2 x 4 … 576! There's no way you ever had one thousand. Plus, you don't have a single empty leg socket."

"I'm still sure Billy the Basher is involved somehow," said Lester.

The chicken waved him off. "Look here. A chart to properly describe a millipede depending on the number of its legs."

The chicken began to read out loud. "A millipede with 520 legs may be called 'millipede–480.' One with 450 legs would be 'millipede–550.' If a millipede has an odd number of legs—which would mean that at least one was lost *and there would be one or more empty sockets*—the rule is to always round down. So 499 legs would be 'millipede–502'. So, you are a 'millipede–424.'"

The chicken got himself another Dead Possum and began to read what young millipedes were not supposed to see. This was all news to him.

Lester said, "Billy ought to be along soon. This trick makes me so angry. I vow to make him pay for it."

The chicken closed the book. "Look, I'm telling you that you are all in one piece. You have every appendage you've always had."

Lester's front doorbell rang. He shouted, "Come on in, Billy. Door's not locked."

The door swung open. A centipede about as thick as one of the chicken's legs scrabbled around the edge of the open door. He had a friendly smile on his large mandibles and wore many different styles, colors, and sizes of sneakers, none of them red. As he passed the couch and spied the disembodied leg, he stopped short. "Whoa, what's this?" he said.

"Lester thinks that's one of his legs," the chicken said.

"Hmm! Nice snack later on? Barbecue, maybe?"

"Shut up, Billy," said Lester. "Maybe we should eat one of your legs."

"Don't get so jumpy," said Billy. "I was only joking."

The Wise Old Chicken cut in. "Boys, boys. Settle down. How about a snort, Billy? Good to get you up and running."

When Billy spied the Dead Possum Scotch, his eyes lit up. The chicken filled a glass all the way, and Billy made short work of it. The chicken set him up again, as well as Lester, who was beginning to smile a little.

Lester took a long draught and held his glass out in a toast. "Billy, I hope you have come to play. No matter what you've done, I am going to wipe the table with your sassy mouth. Hah!"

"Ah, forget him," said the chicken. "Just nerves."

The time had come. All three took their glasses and a fresh bottle of Dead Possum down to Lester's basement. He had a barrel of Ping-Pong balls. The walls were lined with little paddles.

As the competitors began loading up on paddles, the chicken retreated to a side bench where he could guard the bottle and watch.

Table tennis is a furious game when played by multilegged arthropods. According to the rules, the number of paddles used by either opponent must be the same. The number of balls in play is equal to that number. The total number of points to win is 10,001.

Lester and Billy agreed on seventy-four paddles each and seventy-four balls.

The chicken marveled at his friends' skill. Seventy-four balls bounced back and forth in a raging blur. It was impossible to figure out when either won a point. It helped that they called out their score as they played.

Lester: "22." Billy: "855." Lester: "2,183." Billy: "5,627."

The Wise Old Chicken, with a goodly portion of Dead Possum coursing through his veins, began to think about an atom of tungsten. That had 74 electrons zipping around its nucleus in something like fourteen orbital paths. It would be easier to sort out tungsten's electrons than make sense of the crazy melee of flying Ping-Pong balls not more than five feet in front of his beak.

The chicken filled his glass and went back upstairs. A gentle knock came from the front door. When the chicken opened the door he was a bit surprised to see a female millipede waiting there.

"Good afternoon, ma'am," said the chicken.

The millipede explained that she was looking for her husband's leg. He had gotten tangled in a spider's web, severely wrenched a leg socket getting loose, and the leg fell off after he had run away.

When the woman saw the leg on the sofa, she said, "That's it!" Her husband wore a red shoe on his lost leg.

She rubbed the label to clean it. "See?" she said. "Size 1/18. That's what he wore."

The chicken was pleasantly surprised that the 1/18 had been partially covered when he had read "1/16."

The woman took the leg, and the chicken relaxed on the empty couch.

Whenever possible, the old bird enjoyed being a bit of a rascal. When his friends came back upstairs, he would tell them that the leg had simply gotten itself up and walked off. He drank his Dead Possum and waited merrily for their return.

The End

The Wise Old Chicken's Public Lecture Number 1

Regarding unknown archaeological facts of the prehistoric world

They closed the outside lobby doors because every seat in the auditorium was filled. The crowd's murmur trailed off as the MC, a large billy goat named Mr. Barnyard Oats, stepped out onto the stage.

The goat tapped the microphone on the podium. He began, "It brings me great pleasure to introduce tonight's speaker ..."

Then, as though he were announcing a boxer in a prizefight, the goat boomed out one word at a time, each word increasing in volume, lingering, shaking the walls, and echoing among the rafters. "Introducing ... the ... *wise. old. chicken*!"

The crowd went mad, applauded, cheered, and whistled.

The chicken walked out on stage with a serious demeanor. He sorted his notes on the lectern and then looked up, pumping both wings over his head in recognition of all the excitement. He held up one wing to signal silence. The applause faded, then total silence reigned.

The chicken announced, "I would like to begin tonight's discussion with an age-old riddle. Why have pelicans stopped eating squirrels?"

Immediately several hands shot up. The chicken smiled, and, indicating a restless weasel in a middle row, said, "Yes, you."

"I never knew pelicans ate squirrels! Am I missing something?"

Several twitters went through the crowd. The chicken waved his wings. "The weasel makes a valid point. I'm talking here about animals that lived long ago. In prehistoric times."

At this point, a screen unrolled from the ceiling. A light beam speared down from the projector room and placed on the screen a drawing of an ungainly creature that could be called a bird.

It resembled a tall, scrawny dodo. Two elongated appendages, primordial wings, dangled on each side with the tips dragging on the ground, making it look as if their owner had the intellect of a shoe.

"*Pelihogradon*," the chicken announced, tapping the image with a pointer. "The fossil records indicate this creature lived right here, 20 million years ago."

The chicken nodded up to the projector room, and another image appeared on the screen. Four stout legs supported a body in the shape of a Hubbard squash. From the heavy end protruded a bushy stump of a tail. At the front end, two curved fangs hung down past its chin.

"*Squirlothnoticus*," the chicken said. "Better known as the saber-toothed squirrel. Not to be confused with the saber-toothed chipmunk, another species entirely. *Pelihogradon* and *Squirlothnoticus* existed during the same archaeological period, the Pleznotocene."

As the audience digested this information, the chicken paused to light a cigarette. A duckling near the front of the crowd called out sharply, "You shouldn't smoke!" The parents, sitting on either side of the youngster quickly got their offspring under control.

The chicken exhaled smoke and smiled at them. Then he resumed. "This entire area was a shallow inland sea at the beginning of the Pleznotocene …"

Someone rudely interrupted.

"So the squirrels and the pelicans … whatever … swam in this sea? Do we know if it was salt water or fresh? Did the squirrely things and the pelicans try to subdue one another? Drowning perhaps? And *exactly* how long ago did you say all this was?"

All this came from the back row, a distinguished-looking donkey in a trendy brown suit. His mouth turned down imperiously, he puffed a pipe and eased back into his seat with his legs crossed to wait for the chicken's reply.

"Sir!" the chicken said. "Let's not get ahead of ourselves. No one said anything about drowning. I intend to answer all your questions in good time, following the sequence of the fossil record. Will that satisfy you for now ... *sir?*"

The chicken's beady eyes fixed on the donkey like two lasers. The donkey took out his pipe and blushed. He was an esteemed professor at a local college. He looked psychologically damaged as if he wouldn't dare ask another question for the rest of his life.

"As I was about to say," the chicken said, marking each word. "The sea was saltwater and teemed with life. But there were some land animals from the shore that entered the water as well.

"As the water receded, many of the water inhabitants evolved lungs and feet so that they could walk on dry land. One fish species, one that closely resembled the modern bluegill, evolved on land to become a bluegillusodontist. It had teeth like a piranha.

"Being used to swimming in schools in the water, these new creatures hunted in packs. They outran their prey with lightning speed, and hundreds of teeth ripped the flesh off their victims.

"They roamed the forests, snarling, rubbing so hard against trees that their scales ripped off. This must have been painful because the creatures began to howl. A few million years of evolution allowed them to grow much larger and gave them thick fur coats. They became the ancestors of the modern wolves of today."

"You're not telling me I used to be a bluegill!" shouted a wolf in the second row.

The chicken lit another cigarette and said simply, "The fossil record doesn't lie."

"How do you know they howled?" a badger called out. "What, 20 million years ago?"

"You haven't kept up with the latest archaeological methods," the chicken said. "Scientists now can examine microscopic ridges in fossilized mud and determine what sort of noises made them. It is a process known as sonicfractation."

There being no further questions, the chicken resumed.

"Another creature of that age was the *eelorslimikotis*." An image of a creature that was part snake, part fish, and part … *something* popped up on the screen.

"*Eelorslimikotis* did not handle dry land well. They burrowed into the earth for safety. Over time, they evolved into several branches, one being the more dangerous *wormoconstrictus*— creatures that killed their prey like a modern boa. Their fossils are ten feet long, some still wrapped tightly around the central bone of an unknown victim.

"One branch, simply called *wormosaurs*, developed a curious set of appendages. From its top side grew a thin shaft that ended in an eyelet. A similar appendage protruded below, curved so that a sharp barb on the end pointed straight up. These appendages appeared for all the world like a modern fishhook. No one has been able to explain their purpose.

"This species and its strange appendages *decreased* in size over the eons. By the time the creature had diminished to only several inches long, the appendages had totally disappeared. Wormosaurs had become today's earthworms.

"In still another branch of *eelorslimikotis,* the appendages remained intact. The central body diminished over time until it disappeared. Some scientists believe that fishhooks had evolved *long before* man inhabited the earth, that fishhooks evolved right alongside worms."

"That can't be right!" said an otter. "Everyone knows fishhooks are made of steel."

The chicken sighed. "The steel fishhooks today were first made and cleverly distributed as a protective dodge by the living species. Real fishhooks have soft skin striped black and white. If ever one makes its way into your tackle box, please toss it into the water so that it can join its own kind deep in the bottom mud. *Be gentle.* Real fishhooks bleed to death from the slightest injury."

The chicken paused to light yet another cigarette. He noted with relief that the ducks had their young one under control with evil eyes.

"There were other interesting examples of evolution during the Pleznotocene.

"For example, the huge single-clawed *Monoclamponodon*. This was a creature over ten feet long, with a four-foot serrated pincer."

On the screen, the monster looked as though it could cut a human body in half with one snip.

The chicken explained that as the lake began to dry up, this animal was forced to become progressively smaller to adapt to its environment. It became accustomed to fresh water so that it could live in small streams. By this time, it was a mere five inches long.

"As you might have guessed," the chicken said, "the *Monoclamponodon* was the ancestor of today's crayfish. It had to evolve a second claw in order to catch enough of the tiny prey in a brook to sustain itself."

A concerned-looking koala bear said, "I would have thought this would have been the beginning of a lobster."

"No," the chicken said, "the lobster evolved much earlier, from carnivorous coral.

"For some reason, the early lobsters congregated near the bases of unstable underwater mountains. One theory suggests that a favorite form of algae lived in such places. Or, it could be argued that they were simply too stupid to know any better. They had to avoid a constant barrage of boulders, that got dislodged by earthquakes, and came bouncing in underwater slow motion down the mountainsides.

"Often these huge rocks plowed right through a colony of algae-feasting lobsters. Many lobsters were flattened, but managed to survive. Thus evolved the modern crab. The crabs had enough sense to move well away from the hazardous mountains.

"Now," the chicken said, "to the main question of the evening." He coughed, holding his wing politely in front of his beak.

"You're not supposed to smoke." The duckling again! "See, it makes you cough—"

Everyone heard the soft slap on a young face, then a teary voice: "Not s'spose t'smoke …"

"Why *did* pelicans stop eating squirrels?" the chicken said, feeling a bit sorry for the little duck, but otherwise unfazed.

"Numerous fossils of the ancient *Pelihogradon* have been found with the remains of *Squirlothnoticus* skeletons, their positions indicative of fights to the death.

"This primitive bird was easily large enough, and probably dumb enough, to try and prey on the saber-toothed squirrel.

"When a *Pelihogradon* scooped up an unsuspecting *Squirlothnoticus,* it must have been like trying to eat a buzz saw."

The chicken said, "Imagine the wrestling match inside the pelican's bill. The main contender for the bird was its tongue. It was a race to see if the tongue could shove the victim into the bird's gullet, before the squirrel bit off a chunk on the way down or slashed any living tissue it could reach with its fangs."

Here the screen showed an artist's rendition of the scrawny dodo-ish bird hopping about in pain and slapping its head with its useless long wings. A bushy stub protruded from the bird's beak.

"So," said the chicken, "why *did* pelicans stop eating squirrels?

"It's a trick question. Both species simply became extinct. The fossil record comes to a screeching halt. One millennium both creatures were alive and battling one another, the next millennium, both gone!"

An extremely slight aura of disappointment emanated from the crowd.

The chicken gave everyone in the hall a big smile. He didn't care what they thought. He was still at the podium, but in his mind, he was already backstage, tipping back his first big glass of Dead Possum Scotch.

"Mr. Chicken?" said a tiny voice in the very back row. A young skunk had his hand up. "May I please ask one last question?"

"Proceed," the Wise Old Chicken said.

"I was just wondering … well, I … I … Okay, why did the chicken cross the road?"

"To tell you the truth," the Wise Old Chicken said, "I have no idea."

The End

Of Bats and Birds

Robert, a newborn bat, told his mother that he did not like the dark. She was at a loss as to what to do. Her son had been the last one born of all the other mothers. Now they were the only ones left in the cave's remote nursery chamber.

Hundreds of pregnant females had left the colony's main grotto several weeks ago to give birth in the nursery. Each mother nursed her pup and taught it the ways of bats before she could present her offspring to the rest of the colony.

One by one, the mothers finished their work and departed. When only Robert and his mother were left, the nursery fell silent. The only sounds came when either one of the pair fluttered or spoke.

His mother yearned for Robert to change. She wanted to return to the cave's main gallery where bats hung upside down so thickly from the ceiling that the rock above them was hidden from the floor below. Robert didn't care. He was too shy and didn't want to meet any bats from the rest of the colony.

Robert was quite intelligent and had a good sense of humor. He held no one responsible for his circumstances. He had listened to everything his mother had told him so that he already knew all about the ways of bats in the main grotto and outside the cave at night, how they hunted and what they did when they returned.

"What is to be done?" his mother asked out loud. The uneasiness in her voice echoed in the empty nursery chamber.

Robert looked playfully up at her from under one of his wings. He was hiding to be funny. *If he couldn't counter her obvious concerns, might as well try fun*, he thought.

"Don't worry about me, Mom," he said. "I'll be okay, honest."

This did give her some heart. She knew that he was an intelligent boy.

She had to leave him. Nature demanded that she rejoin the colony and her mate, and when the time arrived, she needed to be ready to breed again.

Robert didn't like the dark because he couldn't see in it. It seemed that if he did not echolocate whenever he moved, he bumped into things. It was annoying. Otherwise, he *wasn't* afraid of the dark.

That evening, his mother flitted off to join the others and went with them out to feed during the night. Robert was left hanging upside down on his own. He had a plan, and now his excitement began to grow.

The next morning, after the entire colony had returned to the grotto, Robert dropped from his perch and flew silently past and under the sleeping adults to the cave entrance and out into bright daylight.

At first he flew among the tall trees of a forest. "I'm alone!" he cried out with glee. "All alone, feeling great, and—"

Even under the trees, daylight was brighter than he had bargained for. The light flickered with a hypnotic effect. He had to turn his face down to avoid the flashes as if he were flying into a sandstorm. He was determined to be as unbatlike as possible, so he did not use echolocation.

Half blind, he crashed deeply into a thicket of honeysuckle. The vines entangled all his limbs, but probably spared him worse injury than if he had flown directly into a tree trunk or a stone.

Hanging there, he was able to breathe easily and rest. Slowly his eyes adjusted to the sunlight. He was at the edge of a clearing in the woods.

Wow, was all he could think, looking about, his eyes growing wide.

The daytime world was a beautiful and magnificent place: trees covered in healthy green leaves, a blue sky with puffy white clouds floating overhead, thickets of flowering underbrush, bees hovering and buzzing to touch each little bloom. Behind Robert, moss and lush ferns lit up in shafts of dusty sunlight angling down to the forest floor.

Robert sighed. He felt at home, all alone, far from the dank recesses of the cave, and *all those other bats*.

He was eagerly untangling himself from honeysuckle tendrils when an unexpected melody filled the forest air. It was like bells, tinkling sweetly, pitched low, then high, a brief pause, a twitter, then the same melodic notes began over again.

Robert was intrigued. He spied a strange little creature, about his own size, sitting on a branch nearby. It held a stout little beak to the sky and from this issued the sublime song.

What in the world? he thought. *That's not a bat.*

His usual shyness was gone. He wanted to speak to the pretty little songster. Maybe the light was making him crazy. He was so happy that he didn't care what happened.

"Hello there," he said. "That is a lovely song. By the way, I'm a bat. What sort of animal are you?"

"Idiot bat," the thing said. "I'm a warbler. If you guys didn't hide underground all day, you would know that there are more birds out here than owls and nightjars."

Robert heard this and was taken aback, but pleasantly, not with the awe and fear he felt around other bats. In truth, he was slightly amused.

"I agree," he said. "All that underground business is nonsense. Definitely not for me."

He was amazed at how simply he had responded. He felt good and wanted to continue.

"Bats really don't know much about birds in the daytime," Robert said. Then he added in a crafty tone that surprised him, "Especially ones that sing as sweetly as you."

The bird blushed and looked down. "My name is Eloise," she said. "You're not like any bat I've ever met. I kind of like you."

The bat puffed out his chest. "My name is Robert. I like you too."

"Come on," the bird said. "Follow me."

And with a tiny hop, Eloise took wing and flew off straight through the branches. Robert flitted along behind, his erratic flight easily missing every obstacle in the forest. He was now glad of his echolocation abilities.

Eloise led him to a sunny little glade with a brook flowing through it.

"This is my favorite place," she said.

Solemnly, they told each other their stories of how they had come to be alone, and how now they planned to shun others of their own kind.

Eloise had come into being in a nest with six eggs. All six had hatched, but one poor little sibling was continually pushed to the bottom of the nest. It was a little boy, somewhat smaller than the others. He never could reach the food that their parents brought.

Even at that tender age, Eloise was appalled at what was going on. When she tried to take food down to the little one, the other chicks wrested each morsel from her. As the others grew, Eloise watched the little boy beneath their feet, trampled, then finally silent for good. When the other nestlings grew feathers and flew off on their own, she vowed never to have anything to do with her own kind again.

"Birds may sing pretty songs," she told Robert, "but they can be merciless, and in general, I don't trust them at all. And I have to be careful," she continued. "It is in my nature to sing my songs whether I want to or not. But if I ever hear an answer, I keep quiet and move away. I suppose bats don't sing. That's how you got so close to me. I'm so glad things turned out this way."

So began one of the happiest, albeit more unusual, relationships in the animal kingdom. Robert taught Eloise how to fly like a bat, darting around (though, obviously, she could not use echolocation); and Eloise taught Bobby to fly like a bird, flapping straight ahead at greater speeds.

Spending their days together, Robert and Eloise grew very close—each felt a part of the other. But as time went on, they began to sense that something was missing. Neither knew what it could be.

One day Eloise turned to Robert and hesitated. She looked up at him.

"What is it?" he said.

She took a breath. "I have overheard several other animals that speak of a wise old chicken. If we could find him, he might tell us what we want to know."

At the mention of a third party, Robert's shyness returned, fleetingly, and then was gone. He would do anything for Eloise, hang whatever tried to get in his way.

They flew wide and far, and as luck would have it, they eventually came across the Wise Old Chicken. He was out in a vast meadow, studying grasses and mosses for a new nature book he was writing.

Robert and Eloise landed exactly in his path. The chicken stood there and looked down at them calmly.

They had a long discussion out there in the meadow.

"But you are of different species," the chicken told them for the umpteenth time, as gently as he could.

Both the bat and the bird nodded sadly and wrapped their wings around each other. Robert was stoic and as strong as he could be. Eloise had tears running down both cheeks; her beak quivered.

"I have all the sympathy in the world for you," the chicken said. "I only wish things could be otherwise."

He patted them both on their little heads, let out a heavy sigh, and continued on his way.

Only a few days later, the Wise Old Chicken happened to be passing the same spot in the meadow. Suddenly he stopped. He sensed something amiss in the eddying currents of reality, for want of a better description. He could feel it as easily as anyone else could feel the wind.

He looked up and all around. There wasn't a cloud in the sky. Far to the west, a single dot hung in the air, growing imperceptibly. Way off to the east, another speck flitted every which way as it too slowly got nearer.

The chicken did not know what to think. The two shapes grew nearer, nearer.

Then it dawned on the old bird. *Oh no!* he thought.

When he looked back to the west, something strange happened. The dot had adopted a flitting sort of flight, and in the east, the dancing body had now become a steadily growing dot. Then both shapes resumed their original methods of approach, a steady dot, a dancing shape. Finally, when they were less than one hundred yards apart, both adopted a straight-ahead flight, at the greatest speed. The chicken watched in horror.

"No, Eloise! No, Robert!" The chicken flapped his wings over his head as furiously and as high as he could. But it had little effect.

Robert and Eloise hurtled into each other at full speed. Feathers, fur, and other body parts flew out from the collision. Then what was left fell to the ground with a quiet *plop,* not ten feet from where the chicken stood.

Sadly the chicken went over to observe the remains. There lay a creature that was part bat, part bird. The chicken discerned Eloise's face. It smiled in peace. Robert's partial remains enveloped the bird. They were one now, and they could never be pulled apart again.

"Ah well," sighed the chicken. "I suppose I should have foreseen this. You were both brave souls and had to handle some rough news on your own. But I also know that you were honest, truthful, and loving. You meant no ill toward others. I hope that now you have peace."

The Wise Old Chicken shook his head and wished he could have been a magician, but he wasn't. He was wise, he sensed reality profoundly, but he couldn't change it. He continued on his way. He didn't feel like studying the grasses. Another day perhaps. He walked slowly with a dent in his heart. He couldn't feel the sun on his back. Frankly, he wished it would rain.

The End

Bully Bug

One spring day in the forest, a chunk of soil began to move near the bole of a large oak. Something big as a golf ball was working its way up from below.

Soon two large eyes and a proboscis full of judgment rose far enough from the ground to get a good look around.

"Humph!" the newcomer scoffed.

This was Albert, a cicada nymph. With a grunt, he pulled the rest of his great bulk free. He was a giant, four times the size of other fully grown cicada nymphs.

Albert was famous for his aggressive behavior in the underground tunnels from which he emerged. He flung his weight around only because he was big enough to do it and there was no one to stop him. He said things like, "Say, who do you think yer talkin' to? Yeah? You and what army? So's your old man. What's it to ya. Show me what you got. I'm gonna fix yer wagon but good."

The only ones he might call his friends had toadied up to him in hopes that he would leave them alone. But there was no guarantee. Anyone too close to Albert would eventually endure abuse.

Albert stomped on little ants. He kicked defenseless termites and beat up the smaller cicada nymphs. A few groups of his victims declared they would take no more. Albert punched them until they were black-and-blue.

Albert stood on the open ground and stared up the tree trunk he would climb to shed his nymph exoskeleton and emerge as an adult.

Halfway up the trunk, he came to an irritation that blocked his way. A normal-sized cicada was struggling from its own shell. It should have known better than start molting with Albert around.

Albert pried the unfortunate cicada's feet from the bark and flipped both the cicada and its half-empty shell out into midair, where it hurtled toward the ground. Albert didn't care if it lived or died. It should have kept out of his way. It got what it deserved.

Albert crawled out of his own shell. He waited as his adult body, first a squishy mass, began to harden into a true adult body of monstrous size. Then he called out for anyone to hear, "I am ready to meet the world. If you're smart, keep out of my way."

He did not care for his immediate future. He was supposed to start to buzz to try and attract a mate. Then, in a few weeks, he would be dead.

Great outlook, he told himself.

Death didn't bother him. The sex part terrified him.

Unlike other young male cicadas, he wasn't sure what he was supposed to do with a female. All his life underground, he never had a friend. He had never indulged in "dirty talk" when other boys whispered excitedly about what they were supposed to do.

Albert had no idea how to approach a female, determine if "she's the one," and what to do next. If he didn't perform properly, he would be a laughingstock. Not to mention the shame of not being selected by any female at all. After his shenanigans underground, who wanted him?

In his highly nervous state, Albert found himself unintentionally flexing his tymbals, the drumlike organs on a cicada's abdomen that make the loud buzz to attract females.

His body was firm now, and the resulting sound was so loud that Albert jumped. Nearby a few aphids in the tree bark smirked and spat, trying to hold in their laughter. Albert promptly marched over and gave them all a good working over. Then he turned and swaggered down the bark, savoring the tiny cries of disbelief and pain that he had left behind.

"Albert!" someone said sharply from the ground below.

The Wise Old Chicken stood there, looking up. "Come down here, *now!*" the chicken said.

Albert may have been large, but the chicken was one hundred times his size. Albert slowed to a crawl. His wings were stiff, and he could have flown down much more quickly, but he wasn't sure what he was getting into.

Just then, a buzz from every part of the forest began to fill the air. Thousands of cicadas called for their mates with noise so deafening it undulated in one's head—loudest then less loud then loudest. Simple thoughts were impossible.

The chicken glared at Albert, who was now chicken beak high on the tree trunk and trembling.

"I have no idea why I have been chosen for this," the chicken said, loudly, over the tumult. Then he shouted, "I'm your guide to a mate."

Albert dropped to the ground to get as far from the chicken's beak as he could. He bent back so he could see the old bird's head high above. He was more afraid than ever. "Who's making you do that?" he quavered, barely loud enough to be heard over the buzzing din.

"The Central Committee," the chicken said.

"The what?"

"The leaders of your species. Good heavens, Albert! Have you spent so much time making trouble for everyone else that you have never heard of the Central Committee?

"They know all about you. They know you might not want to have sex. But you owe it to your species."

The bully had been emboldened by all the talk. It indicated that the chicken was not about to eat him.

"You can't avoid it in good conscience," the chicken said.

The hell I can't, Albert thought. He said, "What are you going to do?"

"As little as possible, I'll tell you that. Follow me now. We're going to find you a female."

That did it. Albert spread his wings and began to fly away. Just above the universal buzzing, he could hear the chicken swearing a blue streak.

Albert kept flying until the buzzing cicadas faded to silence.

Ahead of him, the trees stopped abruptly. Albert flew out over a rocky shore against which ocean waves rose and fell with an outgoing tide. Here and there were tidal pools among the stony outcrops.

Albert landed at the edge of the nearest pool. It was no more than two feet across and a foot deep. He spied a school of little translucent fish that had been trapped there by the receding ocean. The fish, each barely an inch long, darted frantically about rocks, barnacles, multicolored corals, and green and gray plants and moss.

When they spied Albert, they immediately came together and looked up at him.

Excellent, Alfred thought. *Just like old times*. He savored the moment before he jumped in.

"You had better be careful, my silly friend!" came a voice directly behind him.

It was the Wise Old Chicken, standing on the rocky shore. The old bird had kept up after all.

"You're way out of your league," the chicken said. "There's more in that water than you think."

There was enough distance between the chicken and Albert that the young cicada knew he could take off and fly out over the water if he needed. His sassy streak returned in full.

"What's it to ya?" Albert yelled to the old bird.

"You don't know what you're getting into," the chicken said.

Albert heard fear in the chicken's voice. Fear made him happy, "brave." He tossed the chicken a finger and dove into the pool.

Albert sank to the bottom and began to walk about. It was bright as day underwater. All kinds of rocks and interesting formations resided in the pool. Ahead of him the school of tiny fish clumped together, looking at the cicada in horror.

"Quick, come this way," they cried.

Their plea baffled Albert. Then the water grew dim as if a cloud had crossed the sun. Albert looked about. A cavern lined with needlelike teeth had moved over him.

Now the little fish made sense. Albert tensed to spring toward them as the cavern closed. He screamed in the dark as the teeth skewered him from top to bottom.

The chicken walked down to the pool and was not surprised that Albert was nowhere to be found.

A puff of gentle air blew over the rocks and swirled around the chicken. Its soft whisper explained what had happened in the pool.

Only a kid, the chicken said to himself. *A woman might have done him some good, calmed him down, made him appreciate there was more to life than harassing everyone you meet.*

The chicken let the little zephyr cool his face a bit until it wafted away. Then he turned and walked back into the woods. He had better things to do.

The End

The Angry Hedgehog

We have always said that we had never met a hedgehog we didn't like. Then we met Oliver Higgins. Oliver was extremely unhappy and had maintained a state of annoyance for much of his life. One could say that he was beyond help. He disagreed with all facets of hedgehogism.

Oliver's personal history reveals how he came to live in constant angst. He came from fractured beginnings. Of the two men she lived with, his mother had no idea which had sired the boy. All three parents had originally fancied themselves hippies, but they got too old for that. By the time Oliver came along, all three adults were hopelessly into drugs.

The trio split, abandoning one another and their half-grown son. They had always assured Oliver that he was a young porcupine. Whether they were joking or, through drug-sodden eyes, truly saw their son ten times bigger than reality, the consequences were the same. They left behind a confused juvenile expecting to live far differently than his hedgehog acquaintances.

Oliver's childhood was lonely. Hedgehogs didn't have foster homes. Though not an adult, Oliver was old enough to join other hedgehogs his approximate age who made their own way to maturity.

To this group, Oliver declared what he had been taught as fact.

He was a porcupine. He boasted that soon he would undergo a growth spurt to become larger, more powerful, fiercer, and braver. The other hedgehogs had better look out!

The others accepted this "wisdom" with a five-pound grain of salt. Oliver wasn't fooling anyone. The others could easily see they were dealing with a hedgehog and nothing else. They heaped derision on Oliver. In a small community, this was the sort of thing that could bedevil an individual till the end of his days.

After several months, Oliver figured out the truth. He was not on the path to porcupine society. Nowhere near it. Some of the other hedgehogs his age had grown markedly bigger than he had.

When Oliver had matured to the point that he realized everyone else thought he was a jerk, he had reconciled himself to the fact that not only was he a hedgehog, but he was a fairly small and meek individual at that. Anger dictated his life. He blamed any problem on the first reason he contrived; there was no one else that he listened to.

Just before coming of age, he determined to leave hedgehog civilization for good. He had grown up in the manicured lawns, hedges, and shrubs behind a row of man-made mansions.

He slipped through the back wrought-iron fence that ran behind the mansions and made his way to the middle of a rough pasture beyond. Here he came upon low and overgrown earthworks of some long-gone hovel that had been built by men.

Pieces of cracked and weathered boards and odd chunks of masonry littered the nearby ground. Brambles and earth covered much of this detritus.

Oliver began to dig his den halfway between this area and the iron fence. He worked with mind-numbing intensity, at first to hollow out a simple hiding place for his own safety. Each day he worked on this project until there were so many forks and secret passages off the main tunnel that if a predator followed him inside, it would run around in circles trying to get a direct whiff of his scent.

On warm, starry nights, Oliver would rest in front of his burrow's entrance. He could hear the happy hedgehog socializing inside the iron fence. Gales of laughter floated across the air. He listened as a witness to sinful and unsavory behavior. Oliver thought that they had too much fun.

Some nights got tricky. He was just off the entrance of his burrow when he suddenly held still as a stone. He watched a silhouette of a dog or a house cat sneak by against the moonlit sky. He had seen badgers as well, nasty brutes that could consume a dozen hedgehogs a day. He watched as owls flew down to settle not twenty feet away, without the slightest wisp of air to betray their presence.

Those nights it was good to disappear down into his labyrinth as soon as he felt it was safe to move. He was not beyond wondering if a cat or an owl had decided to investigate the gaiety inside the fence. Occasionally, screams ripped through the night, and Oliver knew someone had gotten their just desserts.

One night Oliver gave a start. He had emerged from his home to find a tall silhouette waiting for him. It was some kind of bird, towering over him, like a statue blotting the stars.

It might have been a pheasant, maybe a hawk. He flexed his muscles to dive back into his burrow when it spoke.

"Oliver," it said. "You need to lighten up."

As if following the creature's own instructions, a flashlight clicked on. Oliver blinked as the light shot about in the dark. He could see now that a huge rooster held the flashlight. The bird was making sure that he and Oliver were alone in the dark.

Oliver had heard about the Wise Old Chicken and decided that he must be facing the same. What other rooster would be speaking to him and shining a flashlight? He didn't know many details except that the old fellow was often helpful. The bird didn't seem hungry or dangerous. The old chicken's fame and charm won the young hedgehog over. Oliver let down his guard.

"I want to help you reason through all this anger I've heard about," the chicken said.

"What anger?" asked Oliver. He had never considered his animosity against other hedgehogs anything more than his righteous duty and self-preservation.

The chicken answered the young hedgehog with a question of his own. "Why do you live all the way out here, not with the other hedgehogs one hundred yards away?"

"I do not like hedgehogs," said Oliver.

"Son, I am afraid that you have to," the chicken said. "Don't you ever get … urges … Wouldn't you like to be a papa one day?"

"No. I don't want to be a parent. I'm not cruel enough."

The chicken slowly nodded but said nothing. He was visiting Oliver after learning of the boy's past, of the youngster's mean, indifferent, and careless upbringing.

Oliver stared at the ground and wouldn't look up at the chicken. Dealing with such an important presence made him nervous and jittery.

"Oliver," the chicken said, "if I ever needed your help, could I count on you?"

"I guess so."

"Hmm. Not good enough. I need you to be sure."

Oliver thought for a moment. "How would I know you needed help?"

The chicken sensed Oliver's fear. He stroked the hedgehog's back with his wingtip, moving from the bases to the sharp ends of Oliver's quills. The chicken patted Oliver's shoulder.

"That is an intelligent question, my little friend. I get involved in all sorts of … 'incidents.' I try to help others, especially those who need it most. Most times you wouldn't have any idea what I am up to. You'll have to trust your instincts. I believe you have a good heart. You'll know how to help when the time comes."

The chicken straightened up. "Now, would you feel comfortable if I ask for your help?"

"OK," said Oliver. "I'll be happy to help however I can. As long as I understand it, you can count on me."

"Wonderful," said the chicken. "This is very important to me. Thank you very much."

Oliver's jitters were gone. He turned to look at the lawns where he could hear the other hedgehogs in their revelry. They were still not his friends, but they weren't *all* that bad. He realized that he felt a bit sorry for them.

Oliver inhaled long and completely. The air tasted as if it had been laced with powdered sugar. His breath was as good as a long drink of cool water. He had never noticed that before. He had never felt so good, period.

Oliver turned back to the chicken, but the chicken was gone. *I should have known*, thought Oliver. He scurried deep into his burrow and slept soundly till morning.

Weeks went by. Oliver continued to increase the size and complexity of his burrow. If he was going to stay alive so he could help the Wise Old Chicken, the more tunnels and hideaways, the better off he would be. It was satisfying work.

There were plenty of worms, insects, and snails to eat nearby, so Oliver never wandered far. At the end of each day, he relaxed at the entrance to his burrow and enjoyed the late afternoon turning to dusk. The hedgehogs calling inside the iron fence now seemed natural, like birds calling each other to find a mate. He no longer judged any activity. Life was too good and too short.

Never did he forget about his promise to the Wise Old Chicken.

The sun was high in the sky one day when he heard a distant call. It came from the direction of the ancient housing site. First it sounded fairly close. Next time it called from far off as if it were a bird flying close and far. A long pause fit between each set of calls.

As far as Oliver could see, the sky was clear of hawks and owls, and there were no large predators lurking on the ground. He crept in the direction of the old foundation.

"Is anyone there? I'm stuck." It was a female hedgehog's voice, not too far ahead.

"Sally, stay where you are and don't move." This time the voice was not as loud. Its owner called out to someone behind her.

When Oliver got as close as he dared, he called out, softly. "I hear you. I'm a hedgehog."

"At last. Over here!" Then in another direction, "Sally, hold still, it won't be long."

Oliver found a young female hedgehog wedged under an old wooden slat. It was angled slightly so as she had gone under it searching for grubs, the space between the board and the ground became too narrow for her to continue. She was stuck. She couldn't back out because her quills had dug into the wood.

Oliver found a loose scrap of wood to pry up the edge of the board so the young hedgehog could pass through and be free.

"Oh, you angel," she said. She rose up and kissed Oliver square on the mouth. "Wait here," she said. "I'll be right back."

"Wait," Oliver called after her. "I'm Oliver, what's your name?"

"Abby," she shouted over her shoulder.

She returned, leading a young hedgehog, a child not old enough to start school.

"Oliver, this is Sally," Abby said. "Both her parents were killed."

They had been out in the open long enough. Oliver led them back to his burrow, and they went deep inside.

"We'll be safe here," said Oliver.

"Wow, you dug all this?" asked Abby.

Oliver felt his chest swell.

"Could we stay for a few days?" she asked.

Oliver was happy to have them. He was so happy that they never left. He and Abby were fine parents for young Sally, who grew up to be the oldest daughter of several new children, probably the happiest family of hedgehogs there ever was. The burrow rang with laughter to the farthest and tiniest tunnel.

One day Oliver heard a voice from the past. The Wise Old Chicken strode up as if he'd left only yesterday.

"So, my friend," the chicken said, "you seem in good spirits."

Oliver had a thought. "What have you been up to?"

"Now there's a question," the Wise Old Chicken said.

"I was supposed to help you."

The chicken smiled. "That is correct."

Oliver smiled up at the old bird. A thought, just out of reach of his little hedgehog brain, hovered between them. Oliver knew that he would figure it out in time.

"Well, sir," said Oliver. "I'm still ready."

"And I," said the chicken, "will know that I can always count on you."

The End

What the Pepper Wanted

It was a nice place to grow. All the vegetables agreed, from the brassicas (cabbages, broccoli, cauliflowers, etc.) to the carrots and beets and zucchinis and all the rest. Not to mention the happiest row of bell peppers that ever existed.

A lot of sun was the main reason for all the joy. That and meticulous weeding and stirring of the soil and a good watering every few days. If vegetable seed companies ever knew about this place, they would have to go no farther for packet photo ops.

Probably the best feature of the garden came during the night—sleep. After bathing in the sun all day, the cool evenings induced mighty good conditions for this activity. Which was wonderfully quiet sleep, exquisite sleep, sleep that most species on earth could only dream of. The veggies were as serious about keeping quiet as anyone could be. Anyone who accidentally woke them up would discover, much to his misfortune, exactly how angry a gang of veggies could be.

Crickets and toads *were* allowed to produce their soothing chorus.

This wondrous silence affected other beings in various ways. Cats loved it so much that they often fell asleep in a crouch, which prevented the hideous death cries of intended prey. Field mice and other rodents had to tread ever so lightly, particularly among the stalks of corn once the ears began to form ... and the brassicas. Anyone arguing that brassicas do not have ears should remember that brassicas, after all, have heads. Why not have ears?

The orders of quiet extended one night to an aphid who had hopes of joining the Mormon Tabernacle Choir. Aphids were forbidden to sing at night, *all* aphids. It didn't matter that the voice of the aphid in question was treble falsetto and not much louder than a dog whistle. There were *no* exceptions. Any aphid breaking the rule would have to deal with the ladybugs in the morning. As any aphid knew, that would be that!

All night long, the bell in the town hall tower rang out the hour. This was an annoyance the vegetables could not control. They were glad that after 12:00 a.m., the number of rings thankfully dropped to one, then increased by one more as each hour went by, building to six or seven peals when it was high time for decent folk to wake up anyway.

So far we have not mentioned the nighttime problems with the bell peppers. In the exact middle of that row, one young pepper had already grown to a respectable size. It hung down from its stem, all bulging and waxy green, in the cool air a few inches off the ground, its own foliage providing perfect cover above.

Not only did it know that it was a good-sized pepper, but it also had a fairly pompous idea that it was intelligent. The soil covering its roots was smarter. It could be said that this pepper's intellect wasn't going to be probing any waters more profound than a half-dried-up puddle.

As time went by, this young pepper began to have a feeling that something was not quite right. There was something missing; he couldn't put his finger on it (as they say). Each night he became more agitated.

The other peppers could sense the worry in their midst.

"What's the matter?" they asked.

"I wish I knew," the young pepper replied each time in a tearful voice.

He got his answer at 12:00 p.m. that night when the town bell struck its maximum number of times. The weepy pepper cried out, "That's it! That's it!"

In other words, the answer to his worries was now clear as a bell. Even better, the answer *was the* bell.

If I am a bell pepper, then I must be some sort of bell, it reasoned with all its might. He listened as the last tone hung in the air, disappearing into silence, and the crickets and toads got back into rhythm. *So why can't I be rung?*

Then he stumbled across another revelation. *Of course*, he thought. *I don't have a way to strike myself so that my glorious tone could ring out.*

Just then a little mouse came darting down the row, searching (quietly) for the insects that scurried around in the night. It ate these bugs headfirst, to muffle the insects' screams.

The pepper knew the mouse well. They had become friends, as close as any pepper and mouse could ever be. It helped that both were of similar intellect. To mind the regulations for silence they rarely spoke at night above only the slightest whispers. But now, in the pepper's excitement, he slightly forgot this rule.

"Pssst," whispered the pepper urgently, then realized he spoke too loudly.

"Oh, hi," whispered the mouse.

Speaking as softly as he could, the pepper explained what had just occurred to him. The mouse listened intently, sympathetic to the pepper's dilemma.

The two were quiet for a few moments. Then the mouse whispered, "I have an idea! Let me go find a stick so I can tap you with it."

"Great idea," the pepper said out loud, then caught himself.

Somewhere in the vegetable patch came a splurty "Ahem," and then a coughing snore. Somewhere else a cantankerous mumble died away in midsentence.

"Sshhh," the pepper and the mouse said in unison, fearing what had almost happened.

The mouse gave the pepper a tiny thumbs-up and scurried away to find a stick. Soon the mouse returned with a twig in its mouth. If the mouse stood on his hind legs, he could tap the pepper with the twig swung in his front legs.

"This is great!" the pepper whispered. "Do it now, don't wait any longer."

The mouse stood and rose to its full height and gave the twig a mighty swing. The little stick bounced off the pepper with a tiny *plick*.

"No, no," the pepper said. "Do it harder, don't worry about me."

The mouse sighed and took a deep breath. It pulled the stick way behind him and swung as hard as it possibly could. The twig hit the pepper with another tiny sound, *thwock*. Still, nowhere near a ring.

"Hang on, hang on," whispered the mouse. "Let me get a bigger stick and a couple of friends. That could do it. *You stay here*. I'll be right back."

The brainless statement sailed far over the pepper's head. He agreed not to go anywhere.

Presently the mouse was back. True to his word, he brought two friends and a much larger stick.

"OK," the pepper said excitedly, then caught himself and lowered his voice. "Give it all you've got. Don't worry about me. I'm a bell, aren't I?"

The three little mice organized themselves so that they could lever the stick into a rather extreme wind-up position. With three simultaneous little grunts, they swung and struck.

Poik, went the stick against the side of the pepper, not much louder than the twig.

"Do it again," the pepper said.

Ka dunk, went the stick.

"Harder," the pepper cried.

Pwop, was all they got.

"Harrumph! What's going on down there?" one of the other peppers grumbled. "Can't a fellow sleep in peace?"

This aroused other vegetables, who groused and complained.

Our pepper put his finger to his lips to signal the mice to be still.

(We will not complicate our story with explanations of how a pepper can do such things. The important thing to remember is that they all had to be quiet as ... well, mice.)

The mice froze like little statues. The pepper commenced to breathe softly and fake a loud snore. Thankfully, the whole garden was peacefully asleep again.

Suddenly one of the other mice began to jump up and down. "I have an idea. I have a great idea!" it whispered.

The pepper and other mice were all ears.

"I know what the problem is," the mouse said. He explained that they had been using twigs and sticks. No bell clapper was made of wood, at least in their part of the world.

"Remember that old metal spoon we found in the trash? We need to use that! I remember where we hid it."

They were all as excited as could be. It made perfect sense. They all said, "Yes, yes." The pepper nodded gleefully, and the mice ran off.

Soon they were back. They scratched bits of dirt off the metal until the spoon shone.

"Oh, wonderful!" The pepper was ecstatic. He was positive that the spoon, being metal, would do the trick.

Now the mice arranged themselves and held the spoon by its thin stem. They heaved it as far back as they could, and with all three working in unison, swung as hard as they possibly could.

Just then, the village clock tower struck, one time, for now it was that hour in the morning.

"I knew it, I knew it!" the pepper cried out loud.

Even the mice forgot themselves. "Shall we do it again?" they shouted.

"No, no. That did it for me. Don't I sound fantastic?" the pepper fairly shouted.

Up and down the row, all the peppers were fully awake. The older peppers protested the most. The younger ones knew to act as if they were upset. (Secretly they were glad for an adventure.) The baby peppers were the worst. They all began waking up and squalling at the top of their lungs. Nobody could appease them.

This quickly disturbed the rest of the garden. Cabbages woke up and bellowed, cauliflowers screamed, and cucumbers swore at each other. The tomatoes shouted obscenities from their trellises. And worst of all, the beets and carrots woke up and complained from under the ground, shaking their tops angrily, "What in hell is going on up there?" Pandemonium reigned.

Fortunately for the pepper, in all the fuss, nobody knew who started it. The pepper hung there above the mice and beamed.

Just then, a wise old chicken happened by. He had been out late playing poker. Now he was on his way home. The old bird stopped and listened to all the grumpy chatter.

"What now?" the chicken said, rather irritably.

The chicken had a good mind to march right into that garden and give one or two veggies a good peck, or at least give them a stern talking-to. But he couldn't really be bothered. He had had a pretty good night with the cards, and, with jingling pockets, he was in a better mood than usual.

The chicken simply said, "Bah!" Then he continued on his way home, leaving the squabbling garden behind, the home of the happiest and proudest bell pepper in the world.

The End

The Unfortunate Cockroach Experiment

There was once a silly young cockroach that refused to leave his room. He spent all his time in his bed. And when his parents tried to rouse him, he sassed them roundly.

This was all because he was sad. He truly believed he had the most ugly cockroach head of any of his young friends. When he looked in the mirror, he could see that his eyes were like little dots, and too far down on his face. His jaws were tiny and embarrassing, his feelers short, sickly.

He longed to frolic with the other young cockroaches, especially the girls, but that was not to be.

Now his parents had begun to worry. "He needs to get out and run around in the crevices, walls, and germy toilets," his forgiving mother said.

"Today's teenagers, harumph," said his father as he blew on his tea to cool it. "It's certainly not like the way things were when I was that age."

To occupy his time, the young cockroach read magazines and picture books about other cockroaches in the world, many famous, most glamorous. (He even had a couple of copies of *Playroach* hidden under his mattress. His parents didn't know about these.) The magazines helped him to compare his own appearance with all the fine specimens there were, perfect food to feed his self-pity.

One day in his reading, the young cockroach learned an interesting fact. To wit, a cockroach could live just as well without its head … until it starved to death.

That is amazing, he said to himself. He thought about it some more. *Imagine, without my head, nobody will see how ugly I am.*

Now he knew that most cockroaches lived for six months or so, and he wondered if it were possible to eat enough food to sustain him all that time.

Then, as if fate had read his thoughts, he came across an advertisement on the back of one of the magazines. It read: "Roaches, want more zing? Feeling down? Are you lying there dreaming about the garbage cans instead of taking action? Help is here. Try our concentrated cockroach energy pills. Just one gives you the kick to keep going for days. Cheap!"

Wow! thought the cockroach. He filled out the order form as quickly as he could and ran out to put it in the mailbox.

The pills arrived soon after. By then, the young cockroach had devised his entire plan. First, he would eat *all* the pills, enough to keep him jumping well over his six-month life.

Then he devised a sure way to remove his own head. We do not need to get into the gory details about this part of his plan because, well, whatever method would have led to the same outcome.

He ate all the pills and immediately began to feel a building rush. When the moment came to deal with his head, the little cockroach didn't hesitate. And just as his head came off—

Sometime later, after dinner, the little cockroach was scurrying around the room, bumping into nearly everything, and jumping as high as the ceiling allowed about every ten seconds. His parents had never seen him so full of energy.

His mother remarked, "I wonder about our son. He hasn't touched his food. And though it seems he has grown quite clumsy, what a well-behaved child he suddenly is. I don't think I've heard him sass all day."

"That is certainly true," said the father absently, smoking his pipe and pulling his newspaper clear as his son sailed across his lap. "I am still not sure that he listens very well."

When they considered things further, both parents couldn't help but become more concerned. Something was not right with the boy.

They brought their son to the only doctor's office that offered to treat cockroaches. Or, that is to say, an office that had not added "No Roaches" to its sign.

The Wise Old Chicken, MD, was waiting when the parents arrived. The chicken listened, nodding occasionally as the parents went into as much detail as they could to describe their son's maladies. Meanwhile, the little cockroach jumped all around the office like a spring, knocking over file cabinets and chairs, and even causing the papers on the chicken's desk to fly about. *Cockroaches*, the chicken thought. *Got to fix my sign.*

When he was sure that the parents were finished with all their insect yap, the chicken got up and calmly examined the boy while his parents held him down.

With a sigh, the chicken asked, "And you haven't noticed anything at all different about him?"

"Why, no. Tell us what's wrong with him," the parents said, puffing as they struggled to hold him down.

The chicken nodded. Apparently, it was useless to get into more technical details, as in, "My dears, your boy hasn't got a head."

But the chicken said instead, "Take him home. You may have to lead him around a bit, or he may drag you. I'm sure he'll be all right."

Upon hearing this, both parents were greatly relieved. Their home might have been in a continual state of destruction, but it could be truly said that they and their son all lived happily for … a few more weeks.

The End

The Wise Old Chicken Lecture on Petrified Underpants

The audience began to cheer as the house lights dimmed. The Wise Old Chicken made his way across the stage to the podium. While the audience clapped and whistled, the chicken spent a few moments adjusting his glasses and shuffling notes. Then he looked up at the crowd and lifted both wings to signal them to be quiet. The clapping quickly dwindled and then stopped. Except for a muffled discussion between a parent and a child, the hall was silent as a tomb.

"Underpants," the chicken said, then paused to let the word sink in. "Not just any underpants. Giant underpants. *Petrified.*"

One or two in the crowd gasped.

"In a remote area of the Takla Makan Desert, in Western China, high winds have blown the sand clear of a trove of fossilized objects."

Among the artifacts, paleontologists uncovered two elongated slabs, each with the same curious markings on one face.

Behind the chicken, a screen was lowered from the rafters. The chicken picked up a pointer and tapped it on a grainy photo that looked for all the world like a Victorian chest of drawers lying on its back. It dwarfed two men who were brushing debris from its surfaces.

"This is the first of the two," the chicken said. "As you can see, it is in almost perfect shape. However, nothing on it can be moved. The whole thing has been mineralized over the eons, now solid as stone."

The chicken turned back to the crowd. "Next you will see what started this whole controversy."

He turned back to the screen and let out an audible sigh. The image hadn't changed.

The chicken addressed a control room that was above the balcony. "Could we have the second photo, please?"

A new image appeared on the screen. On the left was another of the monoliths, this one with the top broken away. A close-up photo on the right of the screen exposed what looked like a stack of folded cloth. Remnants of the waistband were visible here and there along the edges. No stripes or logos had been preserved.

"The second specimen was fractured, as you see here," the chicken said. "The damage undoubtedly due to early freeze-thaw cycles, when the entire area, a lush forest then, entered a prehistoric Ice Age.

"And here"—the chicken tapped the close-up view of stacked fabric—"are the perfectly preserved remains of eight pairs of ancient underpants."

"Pulleeze!" a ewe called out from the group. She was trying to cover the ears of several lambs huddled against her. "Could you simply refer to these as 'underwear'? Children are present."

The Wise Old Chicken apologized but pointed out that this was a scientific presentation, a discussion of facts. "We must call a spade a spade," he said.

Four young coyotes sitting behind the ewe began to tease her, hissing, "Underpants, underpants, underpants!"

The sheep gathered her children and shooed them quickly up the aisle. The coyotes cackled after her.

"See here," snapped the chicken, "we'll have no more of that."

The coyotes sniggered, kept quiet, but jostled each other with smirks on their faces.

The chicken surveyed the rest of the audience, letting everyone know that he meant business.

"Were they men's or women's underpants?" someone called out.

"What were they for?" another asked. "Who or what wore them?"

The chicken held up both wings until he had silence again.

"We believe," he began, "these underpants were owned by an extinct animal, most likely a legodonth, a creature native only to the area in question …"

"Legodonth?" a fat toad croaked from one of the back rows. "What's that?"

"Ath in 'donth touth my legths'," one of the coyotes giggled.

"One more outburst and you are out," the chicken said, lowering his wing at the sassy group of chortling animals.

The coyotes couldn't handle it. Their bodies shook with mirth, they sputtered through tight lips, tried not to laugh, as tears streamed down from their eyes. Their jostling never stopped.

"Out with them," the chicken ordered.

Four gorillas marched out from behind the stage and straight up the aisle to the now rollicking canines. Without fanfare, each gorilla fetched a giggling brat by the scruff of the neck and dragged him up the aisle. The audience could hear mad guffawing coming from the lobby, suddenly cut off as the outside door closed.

The gorillas lumbered back down the aisle, slowly, looking around with baleful dark eyes. The house was silent. The gorillas retreated the way they had come.

"Are we ready to proceed now?" the chicken asked.

(These lectures were getting to be a real chore, he thought. He should probably up the price of tickets substantially.)

The chicken said, "We were discussing the legodonth."

The audience settled back, ready to listen. *Damn coyotes anyway*, many thought. Though, there were still a few smiles.

The chicken turned once again to the image of the broken dresser on the screen. "Can we please have the legodonth," he said loudly, not even turning around.

The first image of the intact artifact flashed back on the screen. The screen went blank. Then flashed an image of children fishing on a dock, followed quickly by a photo of a fire engine. The correct image finally appeared, only to change back to a blank screen. The image returned and remained still. The chicken slowly shook his head until the projectionist got it right.

"And here, *at last*," the chicken said, "believed to be the fastest animal that ever lived. The legodonth."

The creature had two twenty-five-foot-tall legs. A stout body on top resembled nothing more than a human behind.

The chicken resumed. "Carbon dating of surrounding artifacts tells us that the legodonth reigned over 30 million years ago, during the Implausitene Era, a time when ..."

"Wait a minute," a male June bug in the middle seats called out with a surprisingly booming voice. "If this was a mammal, where are its breasts?" He was sitting next to his wife, who was now glaring at him.

"I never said that this was a mammal," said the chicken. "We have found no indications that it had breasts. No one knows if it was a mammal or not. Some scientists believe the legodonth was a rare example of reptimammilia, a crossover from giant lizards to cows, if you will."

The June bug pressed on. "Did anyone find petrified bras?" His wife now blushed crimson. She did not possess a smiling face.

The chicken, realizing what kind of marital mess he could foster, replied simply, "No. There were no bras."

Changing the subject neatly, the chicken tapped various parts of the image with his pointer. "The legodonth was truly unusual. Here is a modern human to show its relative size."

A man's silhouette stood next to the image for scale. He stood a few feet short of the ungainly creature's knees.

"And here," the chicken said, boldly tapping where the two legs came together, "this …"

"This is where you never want to get sunburned," called out some wag.

"Who said that? *Who said that?*" The chicken glared.

"It wasn't me," called out the same voice.

One gorilla emerged and marched up through the crowd. It pulled a scrawny, wise-assed cat from its seat and carried it to the lobby. This time, strangled cat spits, yowls, and hisses were cut off as the outer door closed. The gorilla returned, frowning and holding its right hand with its left. Blood seeped through its closed fingers.

"Damn cats. Go to the infirmary and have that looked at," the chicken told the gorilla.

"What infirmary?" the gorilla asked.

The chicken puckered his beak. The gorillas, whom the chicken had hired that day, were supposed to act as if the chicken's establishment was more organized than it was. Now this fool had spilled the beans. Of course there was no infirmary.

"Well, have it looked at … somewhere," the chicken said.

The gorilla cocked his head to look up at the chicken, as if to say, *What are you talking about?*

"Just go put some Band-Aids on it," the chicken said curtly.

The gorilla rolled his eyes and disappeared, leaving a spattered trail of blood.

The chicken turned back to the image and tapped again in the same spot, high up between the thighs, this time quite hard.

"Ow! Don't do that!" a mandrill involuntarily exclaimed on the front row, using both hands to cover between his own legs.

"We must be strong," said the chicken. This time he whacked the ancient creature's crotch so hard he almost tore the screen.

"Erf," gasped the mandrill.

The chicken plowed ahead. "As you can see, the legodonth's torso seems to have been not much more than a hinge, to hold the legs together.

"But here is something impressive. Its walking stride was twenty feet long. Running, it cleared almost one hundred feet with each step. Whatever it chased, it caught. Nothing could outrun it."

"What did it do when it caught something?" an iguana asked politely.

"We are not sure," the chicken said, studying the image. "This pronounced vertical divide between its body halves may have been a mouth, or it may have had some other use."

A shiver went through the crowd. It was as if no one wanted any more information on that part of the subject.

"Perhaps it sucked in everything it consumed," the iguana said.

"That may be," said the chicken. "Some scientists aren't sure it had a skull. Its head may have been nothing more than mush, like a big blueberry without a skin.

"At any rate," he continued, tapping the crotch again, "here is where the underpants would have fit, as you can imagine."

Several members of the audience thought out loud,

"How can we be sure of this?"

"There's nothing to hide."

"Why would it wear underpants anyway?"

"We think that it may simply have been a modest creature," the chicken said, "though it ran so fast it's hard to believe anything else would have noticed."

"Maybe the others didn't want to see this leg thing running around naked," a female muskrat said. "Maybe they made it wear underpants, so they didn't have to look at, you know, the thingy."

"You assume it was male? That they were all males?" the chicken asked.

"Not really," the lady muskrat replied. "I don't think you'd ever find a woman running around naked. Not with *those* legs."

"That may well be," the chicken said, staring at the image. "But here is an interesting point."

Again the chicken tapped at the top of the thighs. "On both legs, here"—tap, tap—"we have found indications of damage to the back sides of the bones."

"Something bit it in the crotch?" an alligator called out.

"Perhaps," the chicken said. "Perhaps. But the damage is more consistent with constant pressure being applied."

"You mean whatever attacked closed its mouth and hung on?" the alligator said. "I have an uncle who eats just like that. We think he's disgusting. Do you suppose this legodonth had to go through its entire day with something hanging from its crotch by its teeth?"

"No, we don't think that," said the chicken. "The indications I mentioned may well have come from something far more sinister."

"What? What?" came murmurs around the audience.

The chicken looked all around the room, making sure he had everyone's attention. Then he said in an even voice, "We think it was due to *wedgies*, enormously rough wedgies, day in and day out. There is some thought that the waistband was pulled so far up in the back, it could have squashed the creature's mushy head. That might explain why no skulls have been found."

"Well, if it was me," a bushy-tailed squirrel called out, "and I'm damn sure glad it wasn't me, if I got that kind of treatment, it would be bye-bye, undies."

"Argghh!" the lady muskrat called out. "Then we'd all have to look at you, at your …"

"Beats bone damage," the squirrel countered.

"True," the chicken said. "But it had to wear something. The thing was obviously exposed …"

"Not compared to a mandrill's rump," called out a familiar voice in the very back. One of the coyotes had snuck back in.

The mandrill in the front row jumped up, wearing a trendy pair of boxers that covered everything nicely, all the bright red and blue skin hidden. The mandrill slapped his backside. "Not on my watch," he shouted back.

"Noooo," the lady muskrat said.

A gorilla had already made it to the back row, and the coyote, cackling at its cleverness, was hauled away a second time.

The chicken was exhausted. He had been about to tell them that it was quite possible that legodonths wore underpants even at the beginning of the Implausitene. Just like the squirrel said, the legodonths gave them up because of the rough treatment that the garments allowed. Some paleontologists actually believed that this form of dress dated much further back in time. There was a theory that *Tyrannosaurus rex* himself may have worn underpants. Being such a fierce beast, the *T. rex* might even have invented the wedgie.

"But now you'll never know ... sapheads," the chicken whispered under his breath.

Bad apples ruined the whole barrel. Most barrels contained nothing but bad apples. Just once, the chicken would like to get a dedicated audience, folks who were interested in learning a thing or two.

The Wise Old Chicken always had an ace up his sleeve. He'd had a dozen cases of Dead Possum Scotch delivered before the evening began.

He snapped his wingtip feathers over his head, and, magically, the legodonth image disappeared. The screen rose up into the rafters.

"People," the chicken said, "refreshments will be served in the lobby. Wine and cheese lovers, go to the left. If you prefer boilermakers, go right—just don't get in my way! If you don't want either, you're weird. This lecture is over."

The chicken looked forward to a good, stiff drink, or ten. Imparting knowledge was hard. He sometimes wondered if he had gotten into the wrong business.

The End

The Arrogant Cucumber

As a wise old chicken walked along the vegetable garden of one of his favorite country inns, he heard a deep voice proclaiming, "I am the best, the smartest, strongest, longest, and most handsome!"

Upon hearing this, the chicken stopped to listen.

"I challenge anyone to a test of strength and brains, bring it on!" the voice boomed.

The chicken turned its head slightly, trying to ascertain exactly where the sound was coming from.

"I can dance better than anyone in the world!"

Aha! the chicken thought. The voice emanated from the far side of the garden.

The chicken began to carefully pick his way across row after row of veggies.

The voice grew steadily louder. "I will out-arm-wrestle the strongest of you all. C'mon, who's first?"

All this swagger came from a patch of cucumber vines, the leaves covering everything below in shadow.

"All bow down to me, the fearless!"

The chicken began delicately to part the leaves here and there, finding only infant gherkins sleeping peacefully on the ground, everywhere, dozens of them.

What a bumper crop, the chicken thought. He must congratulate the innkeeper. The chicken wondered if there were any grown yet.

He knew that cucumbers could trick you. While you watched for them all to grow, there is one already full-sized, camouflaged somewhere in the vines and leaves, like a monster zucchini that has become so large and heavy that it has to be winched onto a truck.

"Keep out of my way, world. Here I come!" This time the chicken felt his hackles blown back by the sound. At the same time, he saw a patch of cucumber leaves tremble a step or two ahead.

The chicken pushed his beak down through these leaves and discovered, much to his surprise, a little cucumber, barely three inches long, blabbing his mouth off with the resonance of a town crier. The little fruit grew at the end of an unusually long, loose stem, not straight off the main vine.

"And I guarantee that I will …" the little cucumber thundered, then stopped dead when he saw the chicken peering down at him.

It was as if an out-of-control public emergency speaker had finally quit blaring.

"Son," the chicken said, "what on earth are you going on about?"

"I am the biggest cucumber in this patch!" the cucumber said, rather meekly.

"I suppose that could be true. For now at least," the chicken told him. "But do you know how fast cucumbers grow?"

The little cucumber thought a minute. "No," he said. "Why should I worry about that?"

The chicken, realizing that he was dealing with a youngster (and obviously one with issues), explained as gently as he could that in a few days, any number of the baby cukes all around would begin to swell and lengthen, some much faster than others.

"You are the first one to start growing. Some of the others might grow more quickly. They could become much bigger than you. Just like that." The chicken snapped his wingtip feathers with a loud *click*.

The cucumber kept quiet. He looked at the little gherkins lying quietly all around him.

"And besides," the chicken said, "might be a good idea to lie low. You know what happens to the biggest pickle, don't you?" The chicken drew a wing across its neck.

The Wise Old Chicken really didn't know what happened to the biggest pickle. He simply wanted to provide a humbling possibility for the little fellow to consider.

"They won't get me," the young cucumber countered. "I'm too likable. Why would anyone want to take me from here?"

"Likable?" The chicken rolled his eyes. "If you're so likable, what happened to your tail end?" The chicken was referring to a set of scars on the cuke's blossom end. It looked as if someone had been playing tic-tac-toe.

"Oh, that," said the cucumber. "Japanese beetles. They'll never try it again. I yelled so loud that they flew off. Haven't been back. What do you think of that!"

The chicken didn't answer. He picked his way back across the garden and went toward the nearby inn where he planned to spend the night.

"I am the greatest cucumber in the world!" The public address system had started again. The chicken sighed. It had been a long day. He registered at the inn, ready for supper and a long night's sleep.

Meanwhile, in the veggie garden, the loud little cucumber made two more "announcements" and then stopped. He was now more concerned than he let on. He had had great fun shouting his supposed prowess to the world. But the chicken's advice had not fallen on deaf ears. The cucumber looked all around as far as he could under the vines. He blanched to think of who or what else had been listening.

He wondered about the gherkins. Could any of them truly outgrow him? He could only remember back a few days if that. So how old was *he*? What if after all his announcements to the world, he turned out to be the smallest, weakest, and most insignificant thing that ever hung off a vine?

It would be best to take care of the gherkins now, while they were young and unable to defend themselves.

We need to take an aside, dear reader, to point out some little-known facts. The society of cucumbers is merciless and can become cannibalistic. They often have healed scars or gouges on their skins. These are not always wounds caused by insects, birds, or rodents. Sometimes another cucumber has done the damage. If you ever stroll by a cucumber patch in the evening, don't be surprised if you hear faint snarling at your ankles like the sounds of street dogs fighting in the distance.

The chicken had worried the young cucumber more than ever in his life. The cucumber made a plan. If things got really bad, he would break off his stem and bolt. He would run freely down the road, to live, as they say, happily ever after.

For now the cucumber had decided on more drastic measures. That night he flopped around on his long stem, getting as close as he could to each nearby gherkin. It was easy. He bit through each infant's fragile connection to the main plant, and there was one less competitor for the future. He bit again and again, humming to himself, and the gherkins died without a whimper.

The next morning, the Wise Old Chicken enjoyed a hearty breakfast. He complimented the innkeeper on his cucumber patch. In a week or two, the man would be covered up with fresh cukes.

"Best crop I've ever seen," the innkeeper agreed.

"I'll look forward to a lovely salad next time I stop by," the chicken said.

Outside the inn, the chicken paused for a few moments but heard no ructions from the garden. All was silent. Satisfied that all was well, the chicken shrugged and continued on his way, leaving the garden behind and the sun warm on his back.

Under the cucumber leaves our bloodthirsty little friend surveyed his work of the previous night. Gherkins all around him lay dead, now flabby pods with fuzzy patches of mold already claiming the remains.

But farther off, under the cucumber leaves, he saw many more gherkins he hadn't been able to reach. He had grown to four inches long over the last day or so, and he could see a few of the youngsters that he couldn't reach had begun to grow, one or two already about as large as he had been yesterday.

As the sun went down that evening, the envious little cucumber bit off his own stem so he could travel farther afield, bringing death to every specimen he could find. He carried on his work late into the night.

A few days later, the wise old chicken returned to the inn in the late afternoon. He ordered a steak and a large salad for dinner. He licked his beak, anticipating the fresh cucumbers that he would soon be crunching.

When the food was brought to him, the chicken feasted his eyes on the salad—three types of lettuce, tomatoes, red onions, olives, celery, avocado, and radishes. He found only two mauled halves of a cucumber. On the end of one-half were scars that looked like tic-tac-toe.

The chicken pointed out the sickly cuke to the innkeeper.

The innkeeper shook his head. "Beats me! Best crop we've ever had. Something got in our patch and bit off every one of them. This was the only edible cuke we could find. There was one other, a giant. Found it right next to the one on your plate. But it was too far gone to eat. Eighteen inches long. Probably weighed at least ten pounds."

"Wow," the chicken said, "the one that got away. What do you suppose happened with this one?" The chicken indicated the mauled cucumber on his plate.

"Dogs? Possums? Raccoons? Something had a field day," the innkeeper said.

The chicken thought, *Must have been quite a surprise, my loud little friend, to meet that fellow.*

The chicken enjoyed his meal, even the salad, though he pushed the two shriveled halves of cucumber to the side of his plate. Then he said good night to the innkeeper and went up to bed.

The End

The Raccoon and the Zombie

One day a young raccoon waddled as best he could on his two back legs along a sunlit path in the woods. His gait was hampered because he held the tip of his tail in front of him as high as he could. The raccoon was extremely proud of his tail, and he wanted everyone to see it. He thought the fur on his tail exhibited the epitome of bushiness, the dark rings providing a perfect amount of contrast.

The raccoon had another reason to go to all the trouble of trying to walk holding his tail high. He was sure that if he let his tail point down, the fur and rings would slide off in a heap and be of no more use to him than a pile of old feathers. He would be left with the tail of a rat. Where he got this idea was anybody's guess.

He was on a quest to find the Wise Old Chicken, a legendary bird who was supposed to know everything there was to know about anything. The raccoon wanted to know, rather selfishly, what more he could do to care for his marvelous tail.

As he progressed, the forest grew thick. The sunlight dimmed until you could not see into the surrounding trees and underbrush farther than you could flick a stick with your wrist. The path began to wind so that he could only see about ten paces ahead of him. The air cooled as if he were passing through a swamp.

As the gloom settled in the raccoon came upon an ancient sign, its wood all gray and cracked. It took an effort to decipher an unfortunate bit of news.

"You are now entering Zombie Woods," the sign had once said.

The raccoon stopped and read the message several times, his lips forming the words.

"Zombie Woods?" he thought. "What was this about? Surely the sign did not refer to actual zombies?"

The raccoon looked all around him and thought a moment.

"Nah!" He shook his head. "No such things as zombies. The sign is older than the hills. Whatever used to be here has long gone."

He hurried on. Presently, he came to another sign, just as cracked and ancient as the first.

"Raccoons, beware!" it read.

The raccoon stopped. His eyes grew wide, and he looked all around. He saw nothing but dark, quiet gloom … until a slight crackle of dry twigs made him jump.

"That could be anything," he tried convincing himself. Still, he would just as soon get past this part of the woods. He picked up his pace and waddled faster than before. The quiet sounds kept up with him. The raccoon stopped abruptly and spun around. The rustling stopped. There was nothing to be seen.

The raccoon stood still, not sure what to do. "Who's there?" he called out, his voice an octave higher than normal. His breathing was quick. His heart thudded. He turned to resume his waddle, gripping his tail so hard his fingers were white.

He rounded the next bend and there, not three feet away, stood a diminutive human corpse dressed in filthy rags and struggling to keep its balance as if it were drunk. It was only a couple of feet taller than the raccoon. Its lopsided jaw hung from only one side of a skull that had partially cracked away, exposing a dark rotted brain. The hands were long. Metacarpophalangeal joints consisting only of bone protruding where there was no skin. Two black eye sockets peered at the raccoon.

The raccoon, on his descent from a jump five feet straight up, had let go of his tail. In his panic, he failed to notice that the fur had dropped off and fallen straight to the ground like splinters of lead. The rings fell into a little pile of quoits, several still spinning or rolling across the path and bouncing off into the woods.

The zombie didn't move. It possessed enough grace to hold its head at an angle to keep its loose jaw horizontal.

Another twig snapped in the gloom, and a new rustling began, coming swiftly forward. The raccoon knew that he had only two choices, neither one of them workable: first, he hadn't any toilet paper; second, he definitely needed to see where he could run.

Out of the forest hopped the Wise Old Chicken. He landed on the path directly between the zombie and the raccoon. The chicken looked at the zombie, then turned to look at the raccoon, whose face was frozen in fear, then at the pile of fur and rings on the path.

"What on earth?" the chicken said. He turned to the zombie, saying, "What the hell are you doing here?"

"Couldn't sleep," the zombie said, without taking its gaze off the raccoon. Its jaw didn't move, its voice otherworldly.

"I hate to bring this up," the chicken said, pointing a wing at the zombie, "but what exactly do you not understand? You *are* a zombie! Of course you can't sleep.

"You're supposed to be dead. Get back into those woods and die, damn it!"

The zombie looked down at the chicken. "Couldn't I just …"

"No!" the chicken snapped.

The zombie sighed, then walked off the path into the darkness.

"And take down those stupid signs!" the chicken yelled after him.

"Okay," came a receding reply from the gloom.

The raccoon still hadn't moved. The chicken looked again at the pile of fur and rings on the path and the raccoon's now ratlike tail.

The raccoon followed the chicken's gaze and, for the first time, saw what had happened. "My tail! My tail!" he cried.

"Calm down," the old chicken said. "This isn't the end of the world. Let's find out what's best for you now."

But the raccoon was quite beside himself. The chicken decided it was best to stay with him a while longer. They continued along the path and left the sad little pile of fur and rings behind.

They were surprised to come across the zombie a second time. He was holding both of the old signs and appeared to be waiting respectfully.

"What now!" the chicken demanded.

"Tried to die. Couldn't. Want to apologize. Be friend," the zombie said. "Besides, never liked alone in dark."

The raccoon was not afraid but angry.

"Idiot zombie," the raccoon shouted. "You've made me look like a rat."

"Sorry," the zombie said. "I'm friend."

The chicken gave a heavy sigh. "All right, all right," he told the zombie. "You can come with us. But get rid of those

ridiculous signs. And you'd better be on your best behavior.
Or else!"

The chicken produced an enormous sombrero and handed
it to the zombie. "Wear this," the chicken said. "And keep
your hands out of sight in your pockets. We'll get you proper
clothes soon as we can."

And so, with the zombie's face hidden in the shadows of
the sombrero and his hands dutifully stuck in his pockets, our
merry trio set off. They emerged from the forest and stopped
at the first village they came to. They tossed the signs at the
village dump.

"Listen," the chicken told the raccoon, "here are some
options regarding your tail. One, we buy a coonskin hat and
cut off its tail so we can tape it to yours. I doubt anyone would
notice.

"Bar that—we could go to a vet's and have what's left
cut off to a stub. You could get a prosthesis … or … Wait!
Leave the stump visible and tell folks that you lost your tail
in a war."

"War story," the zombie said. "That very good …"

The raccoon laughed. "Love it," he said.

They bought the zombie a cheap shirt, shoes, a suit, and a pair of gloves. The clothing hung loosely on the zombie's bony frame, but the overall look was passable, just as long as he kept the sombrero in place and the gloves on his hands.

Then they found the veterinarian's office and signed in.

As they waited, the raccoon and the zombie discovered they had some things in common. For instance, they both had relatives in Terre Haute, Indiana, who lived within two blocks of each other. Both loved fast food—crispy tacos with guacamole, the absolute best. They had an unreasonable fear of flying on commuter flights. Each was afraid that the younger, less experienced pilots might crash the plane.

The chicken rolled his eyes and thought, *Why me, Lord? Why me?*

The tail-ectomy was quick and successful: "Snip!" went the vet.

"Ouch!" said the raccoon.

"Ooo!" said the zombie.

"DONE!" said the chicken.

Outside, the chicken couldn't get a word in edgewise as the other two bubbled away. "You will be my aide," the raccoon told the zombie. "Major El Doro von Hinski."

"Like it," the zombie said. "And you. General Beauregard Heyfusse."

Both commenced to concoct their war stories.

The chicken had to go. In less than four hours, he would be a chief judge at a table tennis tournament for extremely aggressive ducks. With those guys, it would not be pleasant if he were late.

So it was that the villagers accepted into their fold two war heroes who lived in a snug little cottage out by the woods. No one was rude enough to look for records of their exploits. The general's missing tail told the whole story.

Later that year, at a Halloween picnic in the town square, a terrific gust blew up. Tablecloths flapped wildly, paper plates learned how to fly, and the major's sombrero lifted off his head and cartwheeled across the grass. When he went chasing

after it, everyone got a good look at him.

"What an excellent zombie mask!" they all said.

The End

Revenge of the King

None of the colony of ants dared go against the queen's instructions for her 100 millionth egg. She had had many a subject put to death for far less. It was always her pleasure to watch her subjects die. Everyone knew it and carried out any request she made, no matter how foul it might be.

"If I have to lie in this goddamned chamber and push out egg after egg after egg, someone's going to pay," she decreed. She determined the "someone" would be the 100 millionth. Many of her attendees lost their lives because they lost count.

She ordered that the helpless egg be rolled against her side where she could jab it sharply with her legs while she ruminated on its ultimate demise.

The egg survived her abuse and hatched into a larva. She would not allow it to be fed more than a single crumb per day.

Other ravenous larvae received all they could eat. The abused larva did not prosper. Soon it was smaller than all the rest.

When the time came for the larva to pupate, the queen ordered the filament of silk intercepted as soon as it issued from the little one's body. A string of workers passed the strand from one to another to keep it clear of other surfaces upon which it could stick. They guided it outside the royal chamber, up the various tunnels to the open ground, where it was rolled into an ever-growing ball. The queen loved to display the results of her malicious deeds.

The larva below remained naked, soft, and vulnerable. It was embarrassing that everyone who cared could watch his unsightly bodily contortions as he underwent all the metamorphoses required to become an adult.

Things did not go according to Nature's plan. Two of its six legs were nothing but wretched stubs, the front right and the rear left. No one knew if the deformity came from constant abuse, or if the Queen had bitten off two legs out of spite.

The crippled dwarf dragged himself clear of the royal chamber and climbed to the surface. As he surveyed the forest from the ground level he was not inclined to stick around. As he hobbled away he could still hear the queen's vile rebukes echoing from her chamber far underground.

"Hah!" she said. "We shall call you Less Legs. Look everyone, there goes Less Legs. Look at him run …" Her voice trailed after him in peals of laughter.

"Mark my words, you old witch," the deformed ant muttered to himself. "I am going to come back. Oh, am I ever coming back!"

The young ant carried on. He knew that no one would follow him. His damaged body was unable to leave a chemical trail. Unless it was a trail of bile. He kept to a well-worn path and soon found himself at the edge of the forest.

The trees ended on a sandy beach that sloped down to lazy waves coming in from the sea. Before committing himself to the open, Less Legs remained in the shadows and carefully surveyed what was before him.

He watched several crabs run down to the edge of the water, only to retreat again, just out of reach of the next wave. He had no idea what they were. They had eight legs and two claws. They turned while still running straight as if they rotated on a turret. Without missing a step, they plucked morsels from the sand and popped the food into their mouths. Their eyes were at the end of two stalks, well above a shell that encased their bodies.

The beach appeared covered with these creatures, all running the same race down to the water and back again.

He did not see the one that had crept into the woods behind him. A claw ten times the length of Less Legs's body gripped one of his legs and dangled him in front of the crab's stalked eyes.

"Mmm," it said. "Look good to eat."

"Wait!" cried Less Legs. "If I look good, just think. There are thousands just like me, not far from here."

"Hmm?" said the crab, his eyes viewing his captive from every possible angle. "Where these you say?"

Less Legs pointed with a free leg back toward the way he had come.

At least one hundred crabs decided to investigate what the ant had said. Their leader, a giant horseshoe crab, broke through the smooth surface of an outgoing wave and strode up the wet sand. Its carapace was a smooth, high dome, dark brown, and it had no eyestalks. Instead, it surveyed the beach with an assortment of eyes that dotted the front and sides of its body.

With Less Legs directing the way from on top of its carapace, the horseshoe led the others into the forest.

The last detail of crabs hauled an old wagon with open casks of seawater. While away from the ocean, the crabs would need to periodically moisten their gills. Failing to do this meant they would not be able to breathe.

By the time the crabs drew close to Less Legs's home, the forest was alive with the news of their arrival. The ants were prepared to fight to the death. Thousands of soldier ants climbed onto one another to build a living ridge across the path of the invaders. Thousands more waited in reserve, ready to swarm into the fray. The workers were prepared to engage the enemy down to the last man.

The ants never had a chance. With Less Legs screaming "Charge," the crabs waded in, snapping their claws and cramming bodies down their gullets. The living ridge of defense proved nothing more than a smorgasbord. Reinforcements were slashed as soon as they grew near.

The rear detail of the crabs pushed the water wagon aside and rushed ahead to get their own fill. The wagon tilted crazily and tipped, spilling its precious cargo of seawater. In the pandemonium of slaughter, nobody noticed the horrible thing that had occurred.

Every ant in the colony was dead. The crabs were silent, busily pushing pieces of their victims into their mouths. From under the ground, the Queen shouted one last indecency.

Less Legs realized that his revenge was at hand. "The Queen!" he shouted. "Dig her up. You've never seen an ant so large."

Several crabs began to dig furiously. They pulled the Queen twisting and complaining into the blinding sunlight.

"Doesn't she look delicious!" cried Less Legs.

One crab held her up as others pulled her squawking body to pieces. Then all the crabs ate.

"Mmm," they said. "This Queen tasty."

When Less Legs hopped off the horseshoe's back, the leader's various eyes studied its passenger. "What sort of ant be you?" it asked.

Without thinking two seconds Less Legs shouted to the sky, "I am the King. Behold! Me! *The King!*"

The horseshoe flipped Less Legs into its mouth. "Mmmm. Queen good. Now King. Good too."

Meanwhile, a wise old chicken followed the path left by the crabs, drawn by the sounds of the carnage. When he came across the upset water wagon, he knew the crabs were in trouble.

The heavy breathing of battle had taken its toll. Everywhere crabs were now on the ground, either gasping for breath or finally silent. The horseshoe held on longest. It imperiously began to make its way back to the wagon when it saw what had happened. The wise old chicken could do nothing as the great crab collapsed and expired.

The chicken knew all about Less Legs and his miserable youth. But he was disappointed in the young ant's intentions. He had caused the death of many innocent brothers simply to feed his appetite for revenge, not to mention trying to save his own miserable life. And that hadn't worked very well.

The chicken stepped onto the battleground and surveyed what was left of the defenders. Ant parts lay everywhere.

Actually, the chicken thought, picking up a sizable remnant in his beak. *I don't mind a nice bit of ant now and again … good for the brain.*

The End

The Bear and the Dentists

An old bear with one tooth, the upper left canine, wandered about the forest in search of a dentist. The bear wanted a dentist for help. Desperately. A cavity in his lone tooth had resulted in a toothache fit for a *Tyrannosaurus rex*.

Presently the bear stopped at the edge of a clearing where a group of several dozen dental students were out looking for bears with bad teeth. Dressed in white coats, some using magnifying glasses, the young interns busily looked under bushes, inspected tree bark, and kept an eye on the sky, in case a bear flew over. Some of the young dentists turned over rocks and logs, poked sticks into rabbit burrows, or called out softly, "Here, bear. Here, bear."

The bear emerged from the woods and stood among the dentists in plain view. They did not see him, so intent were their methods of searching. The bear reared up to its full height and bellowed so thunderously and deeply that the sound would have carried for miles, like a ship's foghorn. This did not affect the dentists.

Just then, the Wise Old Chicken came along and spied the old bear and all the young dentists.

"You need some help?" the chicken asked.

The bear nodded his throbbing and tearful head as he indicated the students working in utter silence. They were too busy to see the chicken as well.

"Follow me," the chicken said. "I know where to go."

The chicken led the bear back into the woods. Deep in the forest, they came across an old hollow log lying on the ground. At the open end of the log was a sign.

"Albert Possum, DDS, will fix all teeth … No tooth too small, too large, too sharp, or too venomous. Eating the dentist *is* illegal!"

They knocked on the log, and out popped a little possum wearing a white coat and a happy smile. He had the bear sit on the log, and after climbing up onto the large animal's shoulder, he was able to examine the cavity in the single tooth.

"Hmm," the possum said. "Okay. Hmm."

Then he ducked back into the hollow log.

The chicken and the bear heard the possum dialing a telephone and overheard bits of the possum's conversation.

"Yes, yes," the possum was saying. "Right away … two should do … usual place …okay … yes …okay … *how much!? … You're kidding, right?* Okay, but absolutely no more!" The possum slammed the phone into its receiver.

The possum scurried back out of the log, carrying his tool kit. He beckoned the bear and chicken to follow him. He led them to a mossy glade where a wide stream flowed. A depression on the stream bank made a perfect woodland dentist chair. Into this the possum sat the bear and prepared his instruments.

In a moment, the underbrush across the stream rustled, and out stepped two of the loveliest young female bears the old bear had ever seen.

Now we have withheld information about the old bear in deference to you, dear reader. No longer can we do so. We assume that you are an adult (or should be, if you are reading this) and have a fair understanding of the world and how it all works.

The fact is that the bear was a dirty old bear. Read, a *very* dirty old bear! He was totally transfixed by the two young females who were now dancing seductively in the stream. They were getting "their fur all wet," as some might say, leaving very little to the imagination. The bear forgot all about the pain in his tooth and drifted into a kaleidoscopic series of fantasies too unacceptable and naughty to be described here. His jaws lapsed into a wondrous, yet leering, smile.

The old chicken watched all this and smiled cunningly. "I applaud you, possum," the chicken said under his breath.

When the bear came to his senses, the females were gone. This was disappointing, but then he realized that his tooth no longer hurt. His tongue felt a smooth filling where the cavity had been.

"Ta daaaa," the possum said and began putting his instruments away.

The bear, the chicken, and the possum all bade each other good day and went their separate ways.

About a week later, the bear was back at the hollow log.

"I think I have another cavity," the bear told the possum.

The possum examined the bear's tooth but found nothing.

"No," the bear said. "It hurts. It'll get worse. I know it will."

The possum stepped back and considered things for a moment. Then it came to him why the bear was back. *"Dirty old fellow,"* the possum thought. *"I guess he's too old to feel shame, though I gotta say those girls do get into their water fun."*

"Okay." The possum sighed and went back into the log to make his phone call.

Down at the mossy glade, everything went just as before. The girl bears came out and frolicked in the stream and got all wet. Watching them intently, the dirty old bear went into his bemused gaze. He felt a tiny nip in his mouth. When he came to, the girls were gone, and the possum announced that he had fixed the "second cavity." Sure enough, with his tongue, the bear could feel a second smooth filling in his tooth, quite near the first.

Week after week the bear returned. He was so regular that the possum was forced to shift his weekly golf outing to accommodate the bear's schedule. This was highly annoying. It meant that the possum lost his coveted midmorning tee time for nothing more than the wiles of a dirty old bear.

The possum found it harder each visit to find room enough between all the previous fillings to install another.

When the bear appeared for his eighteenth visit, our fuzzy little dentist had to explain that there was nowhere left on the bear's tooth to fit another filling.

The bear was so disappointed that he forgot his manners and rose on two legs in anger. Instead of running back into his log, the possum never even looked up. He had been making notes on his clipboard and now calmly tapped his pen on his sign, where it said, "Eating the dentist is illegal!" The bear was God-fearing and law-abiding. He knew rules were meant to be followed. He calmed down and apologized profusely.

"There must be something you can do," the bear said, almost in tears, realizing that his chances of seeing the beautiful females may have come to an end.

"There is one last procedure we could consider," the possum said. "Bend down here and I'll tell you what it is." He lowered his voice and whispered into the bear's ear.

The bear nodded eagerly. "Yes, fine, let's do that!" he said.

"But it won't be the same as the other times," the possum said. "Your tooth will be gone. You won't have any reason to come here again."

Down to the mossy glade, they went. The girls splashed and rolled in the stream. The bear went into his usual trance.

With each filling before the bear had experienced no pain to speak of. He had heard the dentist's tools working gently as if from a distance. This last time was different. The bear felt as if a log grapple was pulling his face off. He awoke immediately and sat bolt upright. He saw the two females heading into the woods.

"Taa daa," the possum said. He held up the bear's much-repaired tooth in some sort of shiny dental torture device.

At first the bear was taken aback. "Now I don't have any teeth."

"Just as I warned you," the possum said. "But not to worry." The possum reached into his tool kit and held up a false bear tooth and a roll of duct tape.

The bear sat back and let the possum tape the false tooth in place. At least now the bear was no worse off tooth-wise than when he had first begun the whole ordeal. He felt renewed in energy—rather peppy, in fact.

The bear thanked the possum and jumped up to splash across the stream and plunge into the forest on the track of the ladies.

Now at this point, since the bear's part of this tale is about done, we will tell you that he caught up with the girls (still wet!) and hit it off quite well with the younger one of them.

Her name was Hermione. She followed him willingly, and they got a room in a motel that conducted business just on the edge of the forest. They locked the door to their room and were not seen again for days.

As for the Wise Old Chicken, there is a bit more to tell. Long after he had left the bear and the possum, even after the bear and Hermione had disappeared into the motel, the chicken found himself passing the clearing where the same dental interns continued their work. The chicken watched for a long time. *Who taught these guys how to hunt for bears?* he wondered.

The chicken passed through the forest and came upon the motel where the bear and the girl had stayed. The old chicken went in and hugged the manager, a dapper young duck named Eduardo, who happened to be the Wise Old Chicken's favorite nephew. They ate supper and, later, around a blazing fire, relived old times over snifters of brandy.

Eduardo told his uncle of an unusual incident not too long ago in his motel. Two bears had come in from the wild for a room. They were obviously a grandfather and a granddaughter. Though it was a bit strange, no one hesitated to rent them a room with a single bed. The staff thought that perhaps bear sensibilities were different than that of humans.

A week went by. The bear had put the room on his credit card, so the motel staff had no worries about getting paid.

But after a second week, everyone began to wonder. They entered the room to see what was going on. The female bear was gone. On the bed lay the body of the old grandfather, a smile on his face and his only tooth dangling from his mouth on a length of duct tape.

What about the dentists? After months of looking for bears, they were getting a bit weary, to say the least.

"Guys," one of them announced, "I don't think this is working out. I doubt there are bears anywhere around here for miles."

The other dentists straightened up and looked at each other. They had failed. Quietly they trudged out of the woods and got into their Mercedes and Porsches and drove off. So discouraged were they that they never came back to these woods again.

Dental schools began offering nonoptional courses on how to find bears. When asked why such learning was required, the faculties refused to answer. The Wise Old Chicken had agreed to keep the secret about it as well.

And, lest we leave any loose end that might fray, deep in the woods, the possum decided that he would become a lawyer on top of his dental work. He fixed up his hollow log and installed a window in front of his desk, so he could watch outside when it rained and feel warm and cuddly indoors. He installed a wall full of those beige books you always see in lawyers' offices. Of course, he never read them. Lastly, just for good measure, he added to his sign: "Eating the lawyer is illegal too."

The End

The Wise Old Chicken
Lecture Number 68-7/8

On the efficacy of zombies, and how their demographics blend with Western markets

When the Wise Old Chicken and his retinue arrived in town, they had their work cut out for them. The local council, being a tad tight with funds, had only offered their old movie house as-is. In this case "as is" was a flexible term that could be wrapped around all sorts of issues. It was stretchy like a weak rubber band.

The old chicken's crew of beavers got right to work on the filthy rows of seats and floors that were particularly "as is." They collected several hundred pounds of stuck gum, dirty popcorn, and candy wrappers. Among the detritus was a substantial number of "as is" squishy items, relics of more strenuous activities than the mere watching of movies. Delicacy prevents further description.

After bagging all of it, including some specimens that appeared to be wonderful habitat for new forms of amoebic life, the beavers disinfected the seats and mopped the floor. The audience could now seat themselves, confident they would not become part of the next outbreak of the Plague.

The restrooms presented another example of "as is," in an inquisitional sort of way. All the facilities were antique but worked fine. Unfortunately, over the years, an unholy stink had settled in that was enough to suffocate anyone who had to use the facilities a few seconds longer than they could hold their breath. Patrons stumbled out, grabbing at the walls, gagging, and otherwise industriously trying to avoid death.

On lecture night, an unusually tall emperor penguin stood guard at the bathroom doors. He wore a hazmat suit with a gas mask slid up over his forehead. A large and easily read stopwatch hung within close reach from his left shoulder.

He kept handy a dolly loaded with two tanks of oxygen. If anyone stayed in the bathroom for more than thirty seconds, the penguin would pull his gas mask down over his face and take the dolly in to see what needed to be done.

Obviously, the Wise Old Chicken was not a happy camper. He was getting tired of all the nonsense he and his crew had to go through just to make things acceptable to his audiences. It all had gotten worse with each stop on his tour. One of these days, he told himself, he was going to give up the whole business of lectures for good. He was really getting to that point.

When the audience was seated, the chicken's master of ceremonies, Mr. Barnyard Oats, one nattily dressed professional goat, walked out onto the stage and held up his two front hooves. He made his announcement over the growing applause: "Get ready to meet the one, the only! Wise Old Chicken!"

The curtain behind him tore and fell from its top supports. It fluffed down onto the struggling animal in a most "as-is" kind of way. The applause tapered to a stop. As the goat wrestled with the heavy fabric, everyone on the right end of the front row heard an angry voice backstage. "Son of a bitch!" it said.

As Mr. Oats shook himself free, someone unseen stage left began to pull the curtain out of sight. The goat gave the slithering fabric a furious kick and stomped off after it, glaciers forming rapidly in his icy stare.

For a moment, no one in the audience spoke. Then a great applause went up. With white and colored spotlights swimming about him, the Wise Old Chicken popped into view. He stood perfectly still behind his podium to allow the applause to live out a full life.

"Zombies," said the chicken once the hall had settled. "Where do they come from? Are they getting more prolific? They certainly show up more in the movies these days.

"Sometimes I wonder," the old chicken said. "If things don't soon change, will these ragged leftovers outnumber us all?"

In one of the front rows, a healthy jackrabbit cried out in dismay, "Arrghhh!" The chicken nodded solemnly.

"Tonight I am going to introduce you to zombie demographics and some surprising ways to make a buck off our dead friends."

The audience comprised two markedly different sorts of individuals. One type, a bit more prevalent than the other, was all unmistakably fuzzy and pink and flush with life. The other type was more difficult to ascertain. They wore wide-brimmed hats or hoodies, their faces hidden in shadows. They all sat together and bundled every inch of their skin in heavy clothing as if winter had arrived.

This group visibly stirred after the chicken's last comment.

"Now let's consider ..." The chicken was cut off by a quavering question from the crowd.

A pretty young piglet, a preteen girl dressed in a fluffy pinafore, asked, "Do demographics involve sex?"

"No...," said the chicken.

The young pig tried again. "Well, can a zombie man and woman … you know … mate?"

Waiting for her answer, the youngster looked about, her face beginning to blush until it was beet red. She sank low into her seat.

"The short answer to *that* question," said the chicken, "is no. Not as far as anyone alive knows." (Note that the old bird didn't say *your* question. He quite understood the flustered state of the young inquisitor.)

The hooded brethren seemed quite agitated. They turned to look at one another. Many lifted their arms and vigorously shook their heads no.

There was a light *thump* as the little pig slid all the way to the floor.

The old chicken got things back on track. "As I was about to demonstrate, zombies have some remarkable demographics compared with the living."

A chart the size of two bedsheets lowered behind the old bird. A capital "Z" titled one side of the chart, "Alive" on the other side. On the "Z" sidebar graphs reached up in several columns, some much higher than the bars on the side for "Alive."

The chicken put on his glasses, picked up a pointer, and tapped the "Z."

"Look, for instance, at average age, gender, sexual orientation—are they straight, or gay …"

A tiny moan from the floor was stifled, out near the piglet's empty seat.

The chicken ignored the sound and carried on. "And education and ethnicity. In all these categories, zombies score about the same as the living, sometimes above."

The chicken tapped more columns. "Disabilities, income, and lifestyle, perhaps not all the same levels, but certainly closer to us than you'd think.

"Take a look at education, residential considerations, and medical problems. We find huge differences. Zombies are by and large much more educated. Probably because they have had more chances to learn, having gone around twice, as it were.

"And look here, residential considerations, enormous contrasts. Zombies don't need houses. The same goes for medical problems. Zombies have plenty of these."

A chipmunk asked in a surprisingly resonant voice, "How will these demographics be most useful?"

"One word," the chicken said. "Marketing!"

A collective sigh went out from the pink members of the crowd. The shrouded members remained still; perhaps a few whispered to one another.

"Here's an example," the chicken said. "Consider this: Everyone knows that zombies do not run well at all. They sort of stagger along. Think of the chiropractic opportunities. Zombies have all sorts of problems with displaced skeletal parts."

A definite stir arose all about the hall, and the hooded members became slightly animated. Subliminal whispers wafted about, none of it making sense to the pink side.

The Wise Old Chicken was on a roll. "Think of treating zombies for hypertension, high cholesterol, diabetes, and enlarged prostates. There is a fortune to be made, and I'll tell you why."

The chicken paused and seemed to take stock of the shrouded members of the audience. By now they were incessantly whispering and gesticulating. The chicken thought, *Bah! They're only zombies. What can they do?*

"Here's why," the chicken announced. "Zombies make the best customers in the world. They have no recourse if they are not satisfied with the service they receive. What can they do, stagger after some medical professional on the belief that a procedure was done wrong, smear zombie guck all over the place?

"Then there's housing! All you need is a small front-end loader and you're good to go.

"A new kind of Olympic Games. Professional sports leagues. All zombie bars. Zombie TV. People, the list just goes on and on."

Now both parts of the audience were completely astir. The little pig climbed back up onto her seat.

"I could build the houses," a large smallmouth bass (or was it a small largemouth, who knows) called out. "I'll just use a shovel!"

"There you go," cried the chicken.

Otters, centipedes, lemurs, beetles, blue-eyed jonquils (jonquils?), pandas, crabs, and weasels. Everyone chimed in with suggestions. The Wise Old Chicken danced about his podium. "Yes, yes," he said. "Now you've got it. That'll work! Great idea there! Wonderful!"

In one motion, all the hooded members of the audience stood and shot the chicken a prolonged and bony bird. They began working their way along the seat rows to the center aisle. The other members of the audience pulled up their knees and held them in their arms and hands so they wouldn't rub against the passing bodies.

Each hooded member moved up the aisle slowly, as if part of a line of dignified monks, out the lobby door, and was gone.

Happy bedlam ensued from the rest of the crowd still in their seats.

The chicken was shouting something in the microphone, but no one could hear him over the tumult.

"Damn it," he was saying. "The most important news of the night."

He looked off stage right for a moment, making little twisting movements with his left wingtip feathers. He tapped the microphone, and the noise of his tapping grew and grew until it sounded like boulders crashing through the roof of a barn.

"People," the chicken announced, blaring above the entire audience. "The bar is officially open. No wine and cheese today. We got plenty Dead Possum Scotch. Anyone wants some stiff drinks, just follow me."

With that, the old bird hopped off the stage and ran up the aisle and through the lobby door. The crowd stood, emptied the rows of seats into the aisle, and followed. Various characters appeared from behind stage left and stage right and ran up the aisle after all the rest. The spotlights switched off.

The entire hall was empty and still.

But for one minor sound. The pretty little piglet made her way to the aisle and looked about. Then, with her pinafore straps bouncing on her shoulders, her little hooves padded downhill and followed the edge of the stage to a lit EXIT sign. She wanted nothing to do with the clamorous crowd. She was a proper little girl, perhaps more curious about sex than some. She took the back entrance to the alley, then ran all the way home to her mom, to tell her everything the young girl had learned.

The End

The Grove That Was Begun with a Gun

Winter and the colder part of spring had gone. It was marvelous to be alive. The forest air was balmy and full of promise.

All through the warm night, crickets chirped and toads trilled. Katydids called from every tree. Katydid, katydid, katydid. One might fancy old-time carpenters using handsaws, drawing back, and cutting down, again and again. Tzeet-a-zeet, tzeet-a-zeet, tzeet-a-zeet.

In the morning, one cicada after another began their prolonged buzz. Thousands more joined in, and continuous choruses rose to a crescendo then settled to brief silence, only to rise up again, perpetual overlapping waves that could enter your head, drive you mad. One had to shout to be heard.

Among this clamor of life, two squirrels chased each other through the trees. The boy, Ignatius, and the girl, Aquilina (their friends called them Iggy and Acqui) were flush with the energy of youth. As they sprang from branch to branch, the leaves bounced, and warm sunlight and cool shade danced on their backs.

They stopped to rest in the outer branches of a tree just beyond the forest edge. Their heavy breathing replaced the woodland sounds, now soft in the distance behind them. Before them lay a dry meadow that stretched to a miniature line of trees on the other side.

The air over this open ground shimmered in the sunlight, as if over a desert. Hummocks of tall, dried grass grew everywhere, surrounded by either bare soil or gnarls of dried ground cover that hung tenaciously to life.

As Iggy and Acqui looked out over the field, a voice called out, "Help me. Someone. Please come help."

Being the more impetuous of the two, Acqui said, "Let's go see who that is!" She turned to race off, but Iggy held her back.

"Wait," he said. "Let's see if we can find out where it's coming from. We might be forever looking on the ground." He didn't bring up what was really on his mind.

After carefully studying the open expanse, they spotted a strange bush. Several naked limbs rose above the surrounding flora, looking like a withered, upturned human hand. There was nothing else like it out there, let alone any other kind of shrub.

The voice called again. "Please help me ... I need help!"

"It's that bush!" Acqui said. "Come on, let's go."

Iggy said, "But what about ... you know."

He didn't say the words, but she knew what he meant. Every young squirrel had been warned about predators, weasels, foxes, and snakes. Even hawks. And owls that never made a sound when they scooped their victims from the ground.

There were no trees in the meadow. The squirrels would have nowhere to climb for safety. The best they could do was hide behind one hummock of grass, then race to the next, hoping the tactic would keep a larger animal confused.

Nothing moved as the young squirrels watched. Of course, nothing would if it were waiting to ambush its next meal.

Regardless, Acqui was on her way. She leaped to the tree trunk and ran to the ground. With a groan, Iggy went after her. One of them had to keep watch.

Beyond the shade, the grassy hummocks towered above them. They ran from clump to clump, stopped, huddled, and looked all around.

"Help me. Please. Oh, please." The voice grew stronger as Iggy and Aqui ventured farther from the trees.

They ran past a rabbit burrow. That boosted Iggy's spirit. The burrow would make a good place to hide. He determined to keep a lookout for more.

But neither squirrel had seen the pair of eyes, two hard beads that had watched as they ran past.

A six-foot snake slithered from the burrow and crept after them. It twisted so quietly among the hummocks that it could have been gliding on a thin layer of air. Its head swayed from side to side, flicking its forked tongue to taste the scent left by our two young adventurers.

When Iggy and Acqui turned to look for danger, the serpent stopped just as quickly, keeping both youngsters pinned in its sight. The snake held so still that the squirrels saw only a crooked stick and didn't give it much thought.

The bush was just ahead, its calls very loud. "Won't somebody help me?" it cried.

Acqui broke their darting pattern and rushed straight toward the bush. Knowing better, Iggy followed her.

They found that the "bush" was, in fact, a clump of roots sticking out of the ground.

"Is somebody up there?" the voice called from below.

"It's all right," Acqui said.

"Are you a bush?" Iggy asked.

"No, a sapling. I was supposed to grow up and become a tree, a redbud."

"What happened?" Acqui asked.

"Mean young foxes, that's what. Pulled me out of the ground for the fun of it! Dug a hole out here and put me in. All my beautiful buds just coming out. Now they're down here where no one will ever see."

The young squirrels were at a loss as to what they could do to help. Their parents had taught them to dig holes, but only deep enough to hide a few acorns or a walnut.

Nevertheless, both began to dig. Just as they bent down a puff of air whiffed their backs. They looked up to see a large hawk, already flying a fair way off. They watched it bank and head back toward them.

The squirrels were petrified. They knew the hawk wouldn't miss a second time. Just as the bird flared, its talons open wide, a deafening crack rang out, like a large firecracker.

The hawk screeched and turned for the trees. It couldn't fly properly and began to sink. The two squirrels watched it tumble to the ground barely fifty feet away.

The Wise Old Chicken emerged from the tall grass with a two-barreled derringer. Smoke swirled from one of the gun's barrels.

Before the astonished squirrels could say anything, the chicken brought up the gun quickly and fired directly at Iggy's feet. Bam! Iggy turned to see just behind him the snake coiling and writhing in its death throes.

"You two had better learn to be more careful," the chicken said as he reached behind the nearest clump and produced a full pail of water. All three splashed water from the bucket onto the redbud's upturned roots. Sounds of relief emanated up to them.

Presently, a group of adult raccoons arrived with shovels and many more buckets of water. They dug until the redbud could be pulled from the ground. Then they put the roots into the fresh hole and filled the hole with water. As the water seeped away, they shoveled the loose soil up to the redbud's thin trunk and tamped down the ground.

The redbud said nothing as the work proceeded. Once properly replanted it took a while to get its bearings. When the sapling came to its senses, it was overjoyed. It began to sob with happiness. Everyone cheered.

The wise old chicken held up his wings. "Those scallywag foxes are in custody, and their parents have all had a stern lecture. The young'uns won't be up to their tricks anytime soon. When they mature, they are going to look back in shame on what they have done."

The raccoons stayed to look after the redbud, and the chicken escorted Iggy and Aqui on their way home. Along the way, the old chicken reloaded the derringer and held it out to the squirrels.

"Take this," the chicken said. "Good protection."

Iggy didn't want it. It was too loud, and it scared him. Aqui didn't like it either. She didn't trust it. The chicken fully understood. He tucked the pistol under his wing.

The chicken knew that his two shots had done more than make loud noises. The incident had already traveled by natural animal telepathy to warn all predators in the meadow of the chicken's terrible exploding wing. The three made it back to the forest without interruption.

Redbud trees make large seed pods that sprout easily and grow fast. In a few years, a thick grove occupied the middle of the meadow.

The trees' real beauty comes in spring. During their last years on earth, Iggy and Aqui would sit high in the forest trees and wonder at the sight of the redbuds in bloom. In the evening, the flowers glow with such an intense electric magenta that they seem to subdue all nearby colors into darkness.

Today everyone calls the trees "the grove that was begun with a gun."

Even the foxes celebrate it.

The End

The Great Hedgehog Wars

"I say, Admiral Fosbie," Henry Prattidare, the unceremoniously deposed Duke of Raspbury, said, "back from Magdelania, are we?"

This account will not deal with the messy business that ousted the duke. He has steadfastly maintained his innocence. "His mistress started the whole thing."

The admiral put down his *Times* and took his pipe from between his teeth. "Quite right, Duke," he said,

Prattidare, lighting his own pipe, said, "Good passing round the Horn?"

Fosbie replied, "Shouldn't wonder if the pond has calmed a bit. Nothing like the old days. Heavy seas rolling the boat to the gunwales, men constantly overboard, loose cannon, fall on your saber. All that sort of thing, eh?"

"Tell me," said Prattidare. "What's this I hear about militant hedgehogs? On the island. What was that all about?"

Fosbie leaned forward. "The devils!" he said. "Did you know they could sting?"

The admiral blinked at his companion. He lifted his snifter for a hearty taste.

This particular drinking glass was the admiral's favorite. It rivaled the size of a goldfish bowl. One could lift it only from the bottom, two fingers on either side of the glass stem.

Moreover, there are sips, and then there are other kinds of sips. The first, gentlemanly, draws barely a few drops at a time. The other kind is more robust and befits a seafaring man. These sips are capable of changing the level of a municipal reservoir. Either way, the glass remains full, thanks to the waiters standing by.

"Sting?" Prattidare said. "This is the first I've heard of *that*."

"Sting like hell," Fosbie said.

"Tell me how they do this stinging business. Have to tread on one, I should think?"

"My dear duke," Fosbie said. "A militant hedgehog on Magdelania could sting whenever it wanted. From a distance of several feet, as well."

Both men sat back and considered each other over their pipes.

The admiral sighed. "Lovely Magdelania. Tourist industry in tatters. Beaches, streets, hotels, all emptier than a mirage in the Sahara. All due to the hedgehogs, you see."

"Absolutely astounding," commented Mr. Prattidare.

"Rather," the admiral said. "It was one of the oddest ordeals I have ever come across. Thank God our chaps had some help."

"I say. How was that?"

Fosbie took out his pipe and grimaced. "Have you ever heard of a character they call the Wise Old Chicken?"

"Egad, who hasn't!" said Prattidare. "Helps practically everyone he meets, hero of the underdog. Incredible what he gets into."

"Not sure we shouldn't take all that with a grain of salt, old boy," Fosbie said. "I mean, how much is one to believe?"

"How could anyone know so frightfully much? He has a good public relations team, I'll warrant. It simply can't *all* be true."

"Tell me, Fosbie, was that glorious bird involved in your caper?"

"I won't lie to you, sir," the admiral said. "I have been told that a wise old chicken was involved. That he was quite helpful. I still don't buy it. *Wise Old Chicken, indeed.*

"I have rather a grim tale, Duke. Are you sure you want the whole story, all the gory details?"

"I simply must," Prattidare said. He sat forward, ready to listen.

"First," Fosbie said, "let's get you a proper drink."

He turned. "Wesley!" he called for the waiter. "A brandy for my friend, if you please."

In a moment, a second snifter arrived, just as large as the admiral's container. Both massive examples of glasswork could scarcely fit on the same table.

The men toasted each other with their miniature oceans of drink.

"Damn fine brandy, Fosbie!" Prattidare said, taking a second "sip."

He sat back to smoke his pipe and let the admiral begin his tale.

"Magdelania had been a peaceful retreat. Coconut palms, sea grapes, pristine white beaches, the sea clear as gin. There were seabirds as well, attractions to any tropical paradise. Pelicans, to name one.

"Then there were hedgehogs. Not native, mind you, stowaways from some other land. Cute little rascals.

"Hedgehogs are not aggressive. And therein lay the problem."

Fosbie took a sip of his brandy. Prattidare made use of the silence to do the same.

"You see," the admiral said, "pelicans soon intuited the pecking order between themselves and the hedgehogs. The birds would scoop the defenseless creatures into their great bills, fly out to sea, and drop their victims into the water to drown. This way, the birds could unroll the poor hedgehogs and eat the soft parts. Bloody shame all round."

It didn't take long before the hedgehog population began to wane. Locals worried about what to do. The hedgehogs had become quite an attraction for visitors. The same could be said of the pelicans. Eradicating the birds was simply out of the question.

Fosbie continued. "A local millionaire came up with a plan to solve the whole dilemma. The man meant well but had no more between his ears than the world's most perfect vacuum. Without consulting anyone, he traveled to South America to see what he could do."

"Why there, I should wonder?" Prattidare said.

"Good thought, old man," Fosbie said. "Fact is, nobody had a clue what he was up to. Chap had his own pilot and aircraft, even a private airstrip. He came and went as he pleased.

"With some skullduggery or other among the natives on the upper reaches of the Amazon, the man came to possess some two dozen of the indigenous hedgehogs.

"This sort of hedgehog had mild venom in their quills. Which meant nothing to the natives. Immune to the poison, you see.

"I'm sure you have read about killer bees in the States," said Fosbie. "Some bright spark had thought it a good idea to breed African bees with the local stock. Look how that turned out." The admiral sat back and drew on his pipe.

"Yes, I know about that," Prattidare said. "Horrid results! And you say this fellow from Magdelania was trying to ..."

"We don't know for sure," Fosbie said from deep within his magnificent snifter. Then he politely emerged. "It all came out much later. Two things occurred that were quite remarkable. The first was what this man brought about with the Magdelanian hedgehog population."

"And the second?" Prattidare asked, before having a plunge of his own.

"I shall tell you that in good time. The entire hedgehog melee was rather astounding in itself. Do let me continue." Fosbie relit his pipe.

Both paused for a long and satisfying sip, preparing themselves to ease back into the story, like lowering oneself into a hot bath after being out on a rainy winter's day. (It was damn good brandy!)

Fosbie continued. "Our man never reckoned changes to the animals as with the killer bee debacle. These were hedgehogs, after all. He simply wanted to see if interbreeding would produce a species that had a bit more backbone, help them with the pelicans, that sort of thing."

"I see," Prattidare said. "And please. Do continue."

After a thoughtful puff, the admiral said, "This blithering idiot had the Amazon creatures set loose at various points around Magdelania. Within three months, a hybrid breed of hedgehog emerged. This species had *drastically* more venomous quills than the South American stock.

"The hybrid became the dominant species," said Fosbie, who was now himself getting a bit pink around the gills. He shook his finger at Prattidare. "And let me tell you, old boy, it didn't take long until they were the only ones! Not a single one of the original species remained!

"Dead pelicans began floating to shore. But not for long. The birds possessed enough mental capacity to pick up on a dangerous lesson: Stop eating hedgehogs!"

Fosbie slapped the table. "Within two weeks, not one pelican would go near a hedgehog, nor anything that looked remotely like one."

"Astounding! Absolutely astounding!" Prattidare said.

"The local hospital began to fill with people," Fosbie said. "A few at death's door, mind you. They displayed large welts on their lower bodies and legs, as if they'd been stung by enormous bees.

"We soon learned the ugly truth. The hybrid hedgehogs had inflicted the wounds. Damndest thing, the tiny creatures were downright dangerous.

"The Island Council quickly determined to eradicate the little scoundrels, every single one. Unfortunately, that was easier said than done."

Prattidare took a dive into his goldfish bowl.

"The thing is," the admiral said, "we soon discovered that the hybrid species was highly intelligent. They possessed a sort of *hive* mentality. They gathered quickly to protect one of their own in distress.

"When our chaps surrounded one of the little beasts, dozens more would arrive within minutes—hidden, mind you. Tiny, angry squeals filled the air. Every man began to get stung, even though they hadn't yet spotted the newcomers.

"As the men jumped back, they could see a multitude of minute spears, arcing in from the surrounding brush, many of them finding their mark on someone's skin. The truth was soon laid bare when the first hedgehog, the one still in sight, picked off one of its quills and, with an angry squeak, hurled its little needle like a javelin into the shin of the nearest man."

The pain of the stings could be intense. Several of the men staggered off in anguish, others ran, a fusillade of tiny quills following like a cloud of sewing pins.

"We tried to lure as many as possible to a suitable spot," the admiral said. "Dispatch many with one blow, you see.

"The plan was no good. Anytime more than two of our chaps gathered, the hedgehogs knew it. The perfect little demons gathered quickly and let loose another hideous storm of stingers.

"The Magdelanians tried poison, only to find cats, dogs, and goats falling sick, their food purposely contaminated by the hedgehogs. Fire was not an option. The island was too small and dry. Many of the houses were right on top of each other."

Both men attended to their brandy.

"The tide certainly changed on all that nonsense," the admiral said. "Several dozen visitors arrived. No one knew precisely where they came from. Little round fellows, no taller than a man's knee, I should say. Dressed in black. Some sort of ninjas, someone said.

"The newcomers were certainly on the ball. They already knew about the island's hedgehog problem. Had come to help, in fact. As soon as they checked into the Grand Hotel and stowed their kits, they got to work. No one gave them much of a chance. Too small, you see.

"We were all happy to find how wrong we were. The little fellows soon showed the hedgehogs who was boss. They were quick! Deflected hedgehog quills with a knife carried in their sash.

"They sprang at a hedgehog, then ducked back. Each lunge delivered a wound. It was simply too fast to see. After several jabs, the recipient rolled onto its back, wiggled its feet in the air, and died. The most extraordinary thing."

"Bravo, I say," said Prattidare. "Tell me, did these fellows get the job done?"

The admiral told the duke that it wasn't easy. A few of the ninjas paid the ultimate price and were carried away by their mates. The hedgehog population certainly began to wane, but the damn things were able to mate quickly and increased their numbers within days.

"Then what was to be done?" Prattidare inquired as he came up from his snifter for air.

With a polite burp, Fosbie continued. "Oddest thing! We received an anonymous wire that revealed a flaw in the hedgehogs' nature. At first, we couldn't believe it. But there it was."

"Who sent the wire?" asked Prattidare. "What did it say, my good man?"

"The leader of the ninjas, we presumed," the admiral said. "Somebody who knew what they were up to."

The duke slapped his hand on the table and raised his voice to an ungentlemanly level. "The Wise Old Chicken!"

"Balderdash," said the admiral. "You know what I think of all that nonsense."

Each regarded the other steadily. Each sipped a good measure of brandy.

Prattidare broke the silence. "Tell me about this flaw you mentioned."

Fosbie hesitated. "We didn't believe it at first. Too damnably simple, though we found it to be true soon enough. We were told that the hedgehogs couldn't stand jokes about politics. Hated such jokes in any way, shape, or form. Quite amazing, when you think about it."

"Political jokes ..." Prattidare said.

"On my oath," Fosbie said. "Awfully strange, one grants that. But bless it all, this advice turned out to be the *absolute* truth."

"Political jokes," Prattidare repeated.

"Damn thing worked!" the admiral said.

"We positioned loudspeakers around the island's perimeter and turned the volume as high as it could go. One ridiculous story after another about inept politicians and governments began to fill Magdelania's air.

"A few were quite funny." Fosbie smiled. "Some folks laughed in the midst of this dreadful business. But most were simply rubbish. Jokes about the Magdelanian Council, the prime minister of Britain, the American president, and, by Jove, the Queen *herself!*"

Being of decent British stock, both men heartily toasted the Queen as soon as she had been named.

Fosbie continued. "Soon a few hedgehogs charged down the beaches, holding their ears and disappearing into the surf. As the onslaught of jokes continued, the few became droves. Hundreds of the little beasts jumped into the surf to be seen no more.

"We kept the blessed nonsense blasting until the beaches were clear. After we turned off the noise, everyone began hunting through the underbrush. Saw nothing. No one stung."

At this point, Prattidare and Fosbie were fairly slumped into their comfortable chairs, holding up their snifters and waving them about as they spoke. They were quiet for several minutes, blinking at each other. It was as if they needed a moment to regain their strength, or to recall where they were in the conversation, or perhaps to remember who the other man was.

Prattidare said, "Hic … Good riddance to bad rubbish!" Then he added, "But you mentioned a second extraordinary thing, Fosbie. What was that?"

"Ah yes, that," Fosbie said. "As things got back to normal, the ninjas checked out of their rooms and trekked in a single file out to the airport. Stout little fellows. Carried their own dead, you see. An extraordinary sight … hic … damn heroic, sad. I followed them.

"The most amazing thing happened as we waited. Several miles away, a large jet hung in the air on final approach. I had never seen such a huge airplane attempt to land on Magdelania's notoriously short runway. I wasn't sure I wanted to watch. But on it came. An A320, unless I miss my guess. The pilot touched down like a feather and stopped with loads of room to spare."

Both men had pulled themselves up straight. Prattidare leaned slightly this way and that, trying not to lose sight of Fosbie, who, while trying to keep a reassuring countenance worthy of his position, weaved noticeably from side to side himself. They each tipped opposite ways, like two slow and unsynchronized metronomes trying to catch up to each other.

Fosbie continued. "The ninjas marched out onto the tarmac. All the little fellows still clad in black, mind you. Ash they climbed the jet stairway … three or four of their black robes … pulled up … jus' a bit. By Jove, *white chicken tails*. We all shaw them."

Immediately, Prattidare said. "Wise Ol' Shicken!"

"Never," Fosbie said.

"Did you get a look at the pilot?" Prattidare asked.

"Only a little white head … sunglasses … Oh my word!"

"Hahaa!" Prattidare said.

"Egad!" said Fosbie.

The End

Interview with
the Chicken

The Wise Old Chicken covets his privacy. His home is unbelievably secluded near the Hollywood Hills. If one stands merely twenty-five feet away, the front door is invisible.

Tour guides drive their vans full of tourists all over the curvy roads of Hollywood Hills and the nearby areas, pointing out the homes of the stars. They pass right by the Wise Old Chicken's abode, yet the famous old bird's name is never called out.

Living quarters are underground. A swimming pool cantilevers into midair from a cliff face in the back. A two-hundred-foot plunge leads to the rugged and untracked landscape below, the habitat of rattlesnakes, coyotes, and the occasional mountain lion.

A camouflaged yet transparent canopy provides protection from the direct sun over the top. Similar fabric covers below the pool. Anyone hiking the foreboding areas below, or flying an airplane low over the top, never sees what is really there.

The chicken invited our reporter, Raven Chadwick (an individual of questionable species), for an interview. One of the chicken's personal staff guided Raven inside the hidden residence.

Raven found the Wise Old Chicken relaxing by his pool, wearing a thick terry cloth robe and reclining in a chaise lounge. He had an old-fashioned glass with two fingers of what looked like scotch and smoked a Gauloise at the end of a long cigarette holder. He wore aviator sunglasses that not many have seen since he usually wears these when he pilots airplanes, of which he owns several.

It was a bright day, and the sun, muted by the fabric, provided a pleasant bone-warming heat over the calm, glassy pool.

"Care for a drink, smoke?" the chicken asked.

"Wouldn't say no to a scotch, thank you," Raven answered.

When the drink arrived, Raven took a sip and grimaced.

"That's Dead Possum Scotch," the chicken said. "Might take some getting used to."

Mr. Chadwick submitted the following report of their interview:

Raven Chadwick (R): What makes you angry?

Wise Old Chicken (C): What really pisses me off?

R: In most of your accounts, you seem hard put to deal with some of the characters that you come across.

C: Two things come to mind.

Number one, individuals who think they are so damn smart, when quite obviously, they are not. It's not easy dealing with a fool. I get quite frustrated. As soon as I am alone again, I kick myself in the butt. I could show you a lot of spur wounds in that territory. Really gets my attention when I hit the bullseye.

Number two, those who get in trouble time and again after they've been advised more than once how to avoid the same mistake.

R: How many individuals have you dealt with that struck you as supremely intelligent?

C: None.

R: As for yourself?

C: Not much different, actually. My favorite saying is, "Real knowledge is to know the extent of one's ignorance." I'm told that Confucius said that around 500 BC.

Man, do I ever have real knowledge.

R: Is there anyone or anything that makes you sad?

C: Yes, creatures that don't know their place in nature. Plus, those that do know where they stand but continue to worry about things they should ignore.

Oh, and most humans. Humans generally make me very sad.

R: Really! What is it with humans?

C: The whole "masters of the earth" nonsense. I think humans have gone way overboard in this notion, and it creates a lot of misery for the rest of the world. Except for me. I am obviously above misery.

R: Now why do you say that?

C: That I'm above misery? Simple, I took a course on misery management and got an A.

R: You went to college?

C: Yes, a good one, the University of Truth and Facts of Life.

R: What did you study?

C: My undergraduate work involved how to learn everything there is to know in the world. It was called "Introduction to Being a Wise Old Beastie."

R: Graduate school?

C: Absolutely. I still had the hefty job actually learning that it is impossible to know everything there is to know in the world. This study was loosely titled, "Wise Old Beasties Never Know Everything." They let you down easy though.

R: Have you ever been helping out with one problem when another situation arises that needs your attention more urgently?

C: Yes, all the time. I suppose, whether I like it or not, I do have a reputation. I hate to put it like this, but trouble follows me around. I wouldn't have it any other way.

R: In that case, how do you manage to solve so many problems? You seem be on top of everything.

C: It only seems that way. I prioritize, address what seems most important first. But I have to keep an open mind to decide what is most important. Sometimes it gets tricky. I mean, if you come across, say, a dog eating a kitten, and a lion is eating the dog at the same time, what do you do first?

R: In a case like that, what would you do?

C: Simple. Get the kitten to start eating the lion.

R: Oh. Which would you prefer to deal with, plants, animals, or humans?

C: It's a toss-up. Humans are the most difficult. I believe they can't get over being helped by a lowly chicken. But since I am the one saving them, they go with the flow. I don't usually get much thanks from a human.

In general, animals are better. They accept their fate on this earth. They can be the most accommodating folks I deal with. Though sometimes not. Animals at the top of the food chain can often be haughty. You've got to watch out. Lucky for me most of them are not trained in martial arts. They never anticipate a chicken being so dangerous.

Plants? Here you can run into some real sassy customers. It's as if they had never been told, or chose to forget, their place on earth, or, more specifically, in the earth. Things can get hectic with unhappy plants. Before you know it, they might uproot themselves and cause all kinds of grief, often at their own peril.

R: I understand that you have spent some time in the United States Diplomatic Corps. How did you like that, and would you say that you were successful at the job?

C: I believe that I did a good job. I have to tell you, though, you run into a lot of pompous people in that line of work. They never could get used to dealing with a mere chicken. That goes for our side as well as theirs. This was the main reason that I left the service. Over the protests of a few US presidents, I might add.

R: Do you smoke?

C: (*Looks at his cigarette, then at Raven and shrugs.*) Yes, I have maintained this foul habit after years of telling myself I would quit. I would like to hear of anyone else who does what I do and doesn't depend on some kind of crutch. One thing I should mention is that smoking has provided me with some fun. Imagine trying to hold a cigarette in your beak, particularly the unfiltered ones that I like. But the sight of all that does not go down well in polite society. I use a cigarette holder.

R: May I ask, what was one of the most dangerous situations that you have ever found yourself in?

C: Here's one. I had been trying to convince an extended family of angry gorillas that they weren't human. They didn't want to hear about it. Too proud, I suppose. One was about to grab my neck and I was about to commence some karate chops that he'd never forget, when a huge bird swooped by and flew off with me in its beak.

I attempted to open a comprehensive discussion with the bird but realized if he opened his beak, I'd be a goner. I saw that he was a kind of huge condor. But not very smart. I learned later that he thought he was a pterodactyl.

At ten thousand feet, we came under antiaircraft fire. The United Jungle Animal Army, UJAA, was under orders to shoot us down. Someone, guess who (the gorillas), had started a rumor that the "pterodactyl" and I were planning to bomb innocent meerkat villages, which was totally false.

The bird made some mighty fancy evasive maneuvers. I was swaying in the breeze, you might say. We didn't get hit because the UJAA were awfully bad shots. They could never afford more than a few extra rounds to practice.

We were coming to the escarpment of the Rift Valley and landed halfway up. Spent a few days there until things settled down.

R: What did you eat on the escarpment?

C: The condor ate several dead animals. I am able to suck protein from the air and subsist on that. But that's no fun. Luckily for me, a fast-food restaurant, I won't mention names, had opened on the escarpment less than a mile away. I would much prefer having a couple of burgers for supper than a lung full of protein.

R: And the gorillas? How did things turn out with them?

C: They were okay. When they realized their mistake about me, they were very apologetic. It is sad to see an apologetic gorilla, especially the old silverbacks. Those old boys were put on this earth to roar and beat their chests. I don't ever want to see one sad again.

R: What was the worst situation you experienced?

C: Worst? You mean another dangerous one or the most humiliating? You know you can't meander all over the countryside to hell and back without stepping in it once in a while.

R: Okay. The most humiliating.

C: (*Chuckles.*) There have been some of those. The best one (I won't say worst, I actually enjoyed some of these times), I had been summoned to a tiny country to be honored by their president. No, I am not going to give you any names.

A limousine picked me up at the airport. It was getting dark, I had terrible jet lag, and I wasn't thinking straight. I asked the driver to take me where the action was. By which I meant the presidency, or whatever they had … Not the other thing.

The limo drove to a dark part of the city, where only a few dim café lights spilled out onto the sidewalk. Ahead I could see neon lights twirling and flashing, kind of like at a Las Vegas casino.

The driver parked in front of several lighted first-floor office windows, behind a line of parked cars that were abreast of the flashing lights. I hopped out before the driver had a chance to open my door, and I walked quickly toward the bright neon entrance.

Inside, a large crowd was dancing. It was a sort of costume party. Hobgoblins danced with fairy princesses, an ostrich danced with an elephant, and a man wearing an old-time powdered wig danced with Wonder Woman.

A group of pixies led me into a room full of unused costumes. I was groggy, getting a little anxious about what they wanted. They fitted me out like a penguin. I suppose my shape kind of matched the outfit.

When we prepared to return to the dance floor, four stern men in dark blue suits intercepted us and took me outside. We went straight back to the lighted office windows I had seen earlier. These windows looked out from the presidential offices.

We went inside, and a dozen dignitaries stood around a long conference table. They lined up, and each shook my hand—the hand of a penguin, mind you.

R: Were they amused?

C: No. I had left my real clothes in the costume room back at the dance hall. The entire ceremony to honor me was conducted for a goofy penguin with a chicken face that looked like a deer caught in the high beams. I *was* honored. But I was also ready to get the hell out of there.

R: Is all that true?

C: The God's honest. Want to see my penguin outfit?

R: No. No. Tell me, then. Another of your most dangerous adventures.

C: Son, you don't give up easily, do you? Let me think, dangerous, dangerous. Well. There've been lots. Mostly encounters with strange creatures that people have never heard of. Freaks, most would say. But I don't look kindly on making fun of species' reproductive misadventures.

One that comes to mind was a run-in I had with a six-legged kangaroo.

R: You said six-legged kangaroo?

C: Six legs. There are a few born every so often. Their mothers won't take care of them. The young ones grow up mean, bullies.

You know how well four-legged kangaroos box? Lightning fists on its two top legs. While you deal with those, the animal balances on its tail and clobbers you with the hefty bottom legs.

Well, the six-legged version has two extra top legs. Try defending against that with only two hands, or fisted wing tips in my case. Adds a whole new meaning to the game. I wasn't sure karate would save me this time. Lucky for me, I was able to talk him down, one hand in my pocket wrapped around my Saturday Night Special, just in case.

R: What about something you could not escape? When you had to go hand-to-hand?

C: Again, it was a creature from the book of exceptions. A chisel-toothed orangutan with hammertoes. Nasty piece of work. But that wasn't hand-to-hand. More like a beak and karate against an angry woodshop.

But the worst? Yeah. Bloodsucking land octopi. They're rare, but when they arrive, they swarm in the treetops, swinging by one tentacle to keep the other four ready for attack. They drop down on their victims en masse.

R: Five-legged?

C: And *blood-sucking*. No one knows much about these creatures because anyone who has ever seen one has probably seen a dozen all at once. The victims are quickly reduced to a skeleton in a floppy bag of skin. You can't play footsie with a land octopus, I'll tell you that.

R: What happened?

C: As I walked under their tree, my ultimate chicken sense gave me enough warning to open my penknife before the first ten or so plopped down onto my head. I can move pretty fast when I have to. I left a couple of dozen octopi writhing and moaning on the ground, at that point wishing they lived in the ocean, no doubt.

R: Have you ever laid eggs?

C: (*Eyes roll.*) I'm a rooster.

R: (*Raven seems slightly confused.*) Oh hell! What am I talking about?

C: (*Smiling.*) I think the Dead Possum Scotch might be working its spell. Want another one?

R: I certainly would. That stuff goes down really well after a time.

A second glass of Dead Possum, quite full, found its way into Raven's hand. He took a long pull and nodded approvingly. Then he had a second and smiled at the chicken for a few moments as if he had forgotten what he was going to say.

C: (*After waiting for his interviewer to say something, anything.*) Next question?

R: Oh. Question. I'll, uh, study my notes.

Raven took yet another hefty swig and riffled through his notebook a few times. He looked up with a slight frown.

R: What did you ask me?

The Wise Old Chicken chuckled to himself, shaking his head.

R: (*In silence Raven Chadwick began to study his watch. This took him a minute or so.*) Oh, I go now.

C: Let's have one of my people drive your car.

R: My car? Did I come in a car?

C: Come back anytime you want. Always glad to meet people.

R: People.

C: Just not humans.

R: Humans.

As a passenger, Raven looked about his own vehicle and decided that it was a nice car. Maybe he should get one just like it. The aroma of Dead Possum hung heavily about him.

The End

Printed in the United States
by Baker & Taylor Publisher Services